The tunnel that runs under the highway had some new graffiti on it. Bry's name and mine were still there, though, up close to the top of the curve. There was traffic on Coast Highway already. I could hear it rumbling over my head and feel the small vibration of loose sand under my feet. Just along that highway a bit…last night…I began running.

Usually I can't wait for the first glimpse of bright blue ocean when I come out of the tunnel gloom. Today I didn't notice. I hurried over the soft cold beach, my eyes blurred. Had Bry felt anything? Had he known, in those last seconds, that this was the end?

———

A SUDDEN SILENCE by Eve Bunting has been named the Sequoyah Young Adult Book Award for 1991. Described as a 'runaway' winner, this award is chosen by Oklahoma students in the seventh through ninth grades.

A SUDDEN SILENCE

Eve Bunting

FAWCETT JUNIPER • NEW YORK

RLI: $\dfrac{\text{VL 5 \& up}}{\text{IL 6 \& up}}$

A Fawcett Juniper Book
Published by Ballantine Books
Copyright © 1988 by Eve Bunting

Library of Congress Catalog Card Number: 87-26969

ISBN 0-449-70362-2

This edition published by arrangement with Harcourt Brace Jovanovich Inc.

Manufactured in the United States of America

First Ballantine Books Edition: March 1990

OPM 29 28 27 26 25 24 23 22 21

For Glenn, who also surfs

1

It was Saturday the 20th of June at 11:30 P.M. when my brother, Bry, was killed. I'll never forget that date, not if I live to be an old, old man. Coast Highway, shadowed between its tall pole lights, the car suddenly behind Bry and me as we walked single file in the thick grass at the highway's edge. The glare of its white beams; the roar as it passed me where I'd dived sideways, belly down; the thud as it hit him. I'll never forget it.

We were on our way home from a party at Wilson Eichler's house and I'd just met Wilson's sister, Chloe, the girl Bry liked. I was walking along there behind my brother, thinking about Chloe, about the way she'd looked in that white minidress with her smooth brown arms and long brown legs. I was wishing Bry hadn't already told me he liked her. I was wishing the Eichlers had moved into the Sapphire Cove house before, last year when I was here in high school instead of this year when I was up at UCLA. I'd never laid eyes on Chloe until tonight, and tonight was too late. Maybe she wasn't exactly Bry's girl, but she was the girl Bry liked. That was enough right there to stop my giving her a second thought. So why was I? *Cut it out, Jesse. Just cut it out.*

Those were the things I was thinking.

Bry was in front of me. Stonewashed Levi's and Levi jacket, brown loafers that were almost identical to mine. Bry thinks I know about things like clothes because I'm older. I was smiling to myself at how long and skinny he was, and how loose he walked, when the too-bright car lights lit up the sky ahead of us. I spun around, saw their blank gleam heading right at us, and I yelled to Bry to jump. I was still yelling as I dived deep into the knee-high grass. Still yelling as the car hit him.

It tossed him into the air, and in slow motion he smashed down on the hood, the car swerving toward the center line, careening back, Bry sliding off into the middle of the highway. The car stopped. I thought the door opened on the driver's side. There was some kind of pause while I lay there in the sudden silence, not believing, knowing I was dreaming, dreaming some awful nightmare dream. Then the car leaped forward again.

More traffic was coming. I could hear it on the highway, and I thought it would hit Bry, too—go over him like some dead, furry animal squashed on the road. I jumped up and ran screaming to stand in front of where Bry lay so still and quiet, waving my arms, pointing down and waving. There was a shriek of brakes as the car stopped.

"Holy cow!" a man's voice said. "What the . . . ?" His head poked out of the driver's window but I was kneeling beside Bry now, with his head in my lap, knowing without anybody telling me that he was dead.

Other cars came. A bunch of teenagers piled out of one and a woman in a camper pulled over on the beach side of the road and gave me a blanket to put over Bry. I put it across his front, which was covered with a wet darkness, but I didn't put it over his face. I stroked his hair. Bry has the worst hair. It sticks up in back and I tried to make it lie down. The man from the camper said he was going to a call box, but the lady would stay with me. I think he must

2

have put out flares, or somebody did, because I saw their orange sizzle and smelled their smoky smell. Bry's head was heavier against me than a head should be, and cars were edging around us now, making the traffic back up, with gawkers leaning out of the windows. A guy was even standing up through his sunroof.

I told Bry not to worry about them. One of his legs was bent funny, and it was important to straighten it. But I couldn't reach. His shoe was gone.

Sirens were coming now, high and shrill above the *slap-slap* of the waves on the beach on the other side of the highway.

"We live just down the road," I told the woman, or I thought I did. "We live in one of the Del Mar trailers, up on the second row. My brother and I were walking on the other side, facing the traffic, and we'd crossed over, because we were almost home. We shouldn't have crossed over." I was babbling, jerking the words out.

"Sh!" the woman said. "It wasn't your fault. You were right up on the grass, off the road. That driver must have been drunk as a skunk."

"Just down there," I said again. "That's where we live."

Later the police asked me all kinds of questions, mostly about the car. What had I seen? Had it slowed? Stopped? Could I remember anything about the way it looked?

We were in Laguna Hills Hospital by then, Mom and Dad and I. We were in a little room that was like an office with carpet on the floor. Bry was somewhere in the hospital, too, probably laid out on one of those steel tables in a cold, blank room with a label around his toe. That's the way it is on TV.

My dad sat at one end of the couch and my mom at the other. There was enough room between them for me, but I stood back against the wall.

"It was just a car," I told the officer. "It was black, maybe, or some dark color. After it . . . after it hit him it went on for a bit and then stopped and then went on. No,

3

I couldn't see the driver. No, I didn't see if there was a passenger. It happened too fast. I don't know."

I didn't know anything except that Bry was dead.

There was a policeman and a policewoman. Neither of them wore uniforms. The woman had on a navy skirt and a pink knit shirt with crossed tennis rackets on the left pocket. Her face was covered with old acne scars, and she told us her name was Officer McMeeken. He wore a blue T-shirt and cords.

"So what you're saying, Jesse . . . the car came round that curve on the highway too fast and too close and you and your brother were clear in, on the grass next to the wire." He was reading back what he'd written already in a black notebook. "And you jumped, and you shouted to him to jump, but he didn't hear you. Why *was* that, Jesse? How far ahead would you say Bry was?"

My father broke in. "Bryan is deaf. Was . . . was deaf. He couldn't have heard Jesse shout."

"Oh." The policeman studied his notebook too carefully. "I'm sorry."

"And I shouted before I jumped myself," I said. Not that it mattered. But they should get it right.

I took the wet, wadded mess of tissues from my pocket and tried to peel one off, tried not to let my mind slide to where it had been a hundred times already tonight. Could I have grabbed Bry in time? Could I have pulled him with me? How far ahead *had* he been? "Now, students, let's consider question number 32: If a car is approaching from the rear at seventy miles an hour and there is a distance of . . ." I got a piece of Kleenex pulled away and blew my nose. There hadn't been time. I'd never have made it. I heard again the awful thud, saw the car stop, saw . . . saw what? Something else that made my heart leap. What? I stared into space.

"I know this is painful for you, Jesse," Officer Valle said, and I wanted to tell her to be quiet, to let me think. But whatever had been there had slid away again, beyond my memory. "We really need to go over this again as

4

quickly and as often as possible, while it's still fresh in your mind. You were at a party in the Eichler house at 2235 Sapphire Cove?"

"Yes." The house where Chloe lived.

"When the party was over, you and Bry decided to walk home."

They were all looking at me.

"Yeah. Jim Lugar gave us a ride to the Eichlers'. He's in school with Bry. The Eichler house isn't that far, but Jim was driving so he picked us up anyway and he was going to bring us back." I glanced at her and quickly away.

"Now let me get the geography straight here. Sapphire Cove is a community on the bluff, south of your trailer park and on the other side of the highway?"

"Right. And Clambake Point is at the end of Sapphire Cove Road."

"So after the party, you and Bry walked down the road onto the highway and proceeded north on that side, facing the traffic until . . ."

"Until we ran across. The highway was clear and we could see our own gates." Actually, Bry had raced across ahead of me and I'd followed him, but I didn't say that.

She had a notebook, too, that she read from. "Isn't there a pedestrian tunnel under the highway that leads right into your park?"

"Yes. But it's longer to go that way. You have to double back." I swallowed. "I wish we had."

"OK Jesse. I know this is bad." There was sympathy in Officer Valle's voice. For the first time I noticed how kind and warm her dark eyes were. "The Eichler parents weren't home?"

"No. They were coming home later. I think they'd gone to some do of their own in Newport. This was a last-minute kind of party."

"Tell me about it."

"Well, there was a fair amount of beer and . . . and other stuff."

I remembered Wilson Eichler making a castle of champagne glasses on the kitchen counter, pouring some kind of booze into the top one, letting it spill over to fill the glasses underneath. Sharon Fields had lapped up the overflow. I remembered Pat Shepherd with sheets from Mrs. Eichler's linen closet tied round him, a pillow case on his head, yelling, "Who ya gonna call? Who ya gonna call? Ghostbusters!" Jim Lugar had been completely spaced, flat out on a couch, high as an asteroid. I remembered Chloe looking down at him, wrinkling her nose. "Stoned out of his head," she'd said. I remembered Bry, leaning forward a little, staring at Chloe's lips the way he does. Bry lip-reads so well you can hardly tell he's deaf. I remembered thinking, *I wish I could stare at her lips like that.*

"We'll have to get them all out of here before my parents come home," she'd said.

I'd lifted Lugar's limp hand and let it drop. "One thing for sure, he's not giving us any ride."

"Is he a friend of yours?"

"Not particularly."

"Then you've got better taste than my brother. I am so mad at him and his so-called party that I can't even see straight."

Bry had touched her arm and smiled and I could tell he'd missed some of what she'd said.

"Chloe's a great surfer, did I tell you, Jess? She's super-grade number one. My brother here's good, too."

"Oh, yeah?" Chloe's blue, shadow-lashed eyes met mine with a flicker of interest. "You surf in the cove?"

"Some," I said. "Mostly I go over to Trestles." Already I was thinking that if *she* surfed the cove, maybe I should, too.

"Are you going to White Sands on the Fourth?" she asked. Fourth of July is always the big White Sands All-Pro Surfing Championship Finals.

"For sure," I said. "I wouldn't miss it. How about you?" She'd nodded.

I was amazed at how good I felt knowing I'd see her

6

again at least once, on the Fourth. "Bry and I go every year," I'd said.

But he wouldn't be going this year.

Officer Valle was still talking. "So I'm to presume this Jim Lugar had too much to drink and you and Bry made the decision to walk home."

"Yes." I jerked my head back and forth like a chicken, watching her, watching Mom and Dad, watching the other cop, who stood looking out of the window. "Who would have thought . . ." I said. "I mean, we thought we'd be safer, walking."

"It was the right decision, Jesse," Dad said.

"I could have called you," I began. "I should have."

Officer Valle interrupted. "You probably didn't want to disturb your parents that late, right Jesse?"

"Right. I guess we figured they'd be in bed."

They had been in bed. The police had wakened them when they'd brought me home. At first Dad had looked more puzzled than frightened, and he'd said, "Jesse? What's wrong?" And then he'd looked behind, where I stood sniffling and shivering, and he'd said, "Where's Bry? Has something happened to him?"

I got a sudden cramp in my stomach, remembering. Was there a bathroom around here somewhere?

"Do you think the driver who hit my son was drunk?" Mom asked Officer Valle.

"It looks as if that might be a possibility, ma'am. He certainly lost control of his vehicle. We can tell that by the skid marks."

"You can't remember anything about the license plates, Jesse?" Officer McMeeken asked. "Were they white with blue letters? Blue, maybe, with yellow letters?"

I shook my head. "It went by so fast. I guess when it stopped I was close enough to read them. But I was looking at Bry." I bent over, holding the cramp in.

"That boy who took you—Lugar? You don't think he could have wakened and come after you?"

7

"He has a red Mustang," I said. "It wasn't a red Mustang. And he wasn't about to waken."

"Well, somebody else who was there. Somebody who knew you were walking and . . ."

"I don't think so. The car was too . . ." I struggled for the word I wanted. "Too expensive. Not real big like a limousine, but luxurious, or fancy or . . . None of the kids I know drives a car like that."

"If you can think of anything, Jesse. Anything."

I shook my head numbly. But there was a small, flashing signal at the edge of my brain. I had seen something. What?

2

NONE OF US went to bed the night Bry was killed. We sat, huddled together in the living room, going over and over what had happened. Dad called all our relatives—our grandparents in Minnesota, Aunt Lila and Uncle Fred. I don't know how he did that. I felt so sorry for him, having to tell them. Sorry for them, for all of us. I gnawed at my fingers, living and reliving those awful last seconds. If only, if only . . .

At five in the morning I slipped away to my room and put on my wet suit.

Surfing has always been one of my major comforts. There's something about sitting out there on my board, way early, before the sun comes up and the world is just beginning, that brings a kind of peace. Ever since I can remember I've surfed in the mornings, sneaking past Bry's room so he wouldn't sense me there and tag along. I was sneaking past this first morning when it hit me all over again. Bry wouldn't tag along behind me again. Ever.

I opened his closed door. The bed wasn't made. There was still a dent in the pillow. On the desk was a scattering

9

of white cardboard cutouts. He'd probably been in the middle of making something. A flannel shirt lay in a rumple beside the bed. I picked it up, folded it, and jammed it into a drawer. I closed the door carefully behind me.

Mom had gone outside. She was sitting all by herself in the wicker chair on the deck staring at nothing. Or maybe she was staring at the bird feeder by the hedge, or seeing through the hedge, beyond it, over the trailer roofs and trees to the gray stretch of highway.

"Mom?" I said softly. "I'm going surfing for a little while. What time does Grandma's plane get in?"

She didn't answer.

"Mom?" I put down my board and went toward her and touched her shoulder.

"I loved him so much, Jesse," she said in a dead kind of voice.

"I know." I knelt and put my arms around her, and we were rocking back and forth, both of us crying and moaning.

"Your father wanted me to have an abortion, you know, when I was pregnant and got the German measles. There was always the chance there would be something wrong with the baby."

"Sh!" I whispered. "Just sh."

"I wouldn't even go for the tests. I'm glad I didn't, though. It's better. Bry had sixteen good years, didn't he, Jesse?"

"Yes, Mom. He was great."

"But if he hadn't been deaf, he'd have heard when you yelled at him, Jesse. He'd still be alive."

"Mom! Stop it!" I cradled her head against my wet suit and put a hand over her ear so she wouldn't hear what she was saying. I wished I couldn't hear what I was thinking. If I'd just jumped forward instead of sideways. If I'd taken him to safety with me. "How far ahead would you say Bry was?" Officer McMeeken had asked. *How far?*

Mom pulled herself gently away, fished a Kleenex out of the pocket of her robe, and blew her nose. I couldn't believe her face. It was puffy and covered with little red

10

marks. Her eyes seemed to have disappeared into the flesh around them.

"Do you want a cup of coffee? I'm going to make a pot. Her voice seemed more normal. "Your father will need some. He went up to the gazebo a while ago. I think he needed to be alone." I nodded. The gazebo, perched right on the edge of our high green, is a good place to go to be alone. You could be almost as alone there as out on the ocean.

Once I'd found Bry up in the gazebo. He was about eight at the time, and he was smashing at the wooden walls and seats with the Basher Club Aunt Lila had brought for him. The Basher is Styrofoam and can't hurt anything, even if you use it to bash yourself. I remember how Bry had been saying words, not accurately but close, words you wouldn't think a kid would know, especially a deaf kid. And I understood how rotten things were for him a lot of the time, and how he kept it to himself. He hadn't heard me coming, of course, and he didn't hear me leave.

I never forgot Bry in that gazebo.

And that's where my father was now. He could probably have used the Basher, too.

Mom stood up. "I need to get started anyway. There are things I have to do. Aunt Lila said they'd stay in the Coast Motel, so we wouldn't have to . . . I mean, there *is* the bed . . . I mean . . ." She was talking about Bry's bed. He and I always shared my room when any of the relatives came.

"No," I said. "No, no, no."

She sank down again. "They understood. They loved him, too. They wouldn't want his room."

"Look." I put my hands one on each arm of her chair, my face close to hers. "I'll help you. What do we have to do? Cook, or what?"

She sighed. "Nothing. Really. Go surfing, baby." She closed her eyes. "I think I'll just sit here for a while."

I edged back and stood against the side of the trailer, watching her. In a few minutes, when her hands unclenched

11

and her breathing got heavier and I knew she slept, I picked up my board and left for the ocean.

The tunnel that runs under the highway had some new graffiti on it. Bry's name and mine were still there, though, up close to the top curve. So was my friend Alexander's. I remembered when we'd put our names there, me on Alexander's shoulders, Bry on mine, all of us staggering around and Bry trying to write with the spray can. Alexander is real strong. Alex the Ox we call him. God, he wouldn't even know about Bry yet. Hardly anybody would know.

There was traffic on Coast Highway already. I could hear it rumbling over my head and feel the small vibration of loose sand under my feet. Just along that highway a bit . . . last night . . . I began running. It's hard to run with your board.

Usually I can't wait for that first glimpse of bright blue ocean when I come out of the tunnel gloom. Today I didn't notice. I hurried over the soft, cold beach, my eyes blurred. Had Bry felt anything? Had he known, in those last seconds, that this was the end?

My breath was coming in great burning gasps as I ran toward the ocean and some sort of easing of the

But the easing didn't come. I sat on my board between the blueness of sea and sky and I was crying again, though I hadn't known there were tears left. A diver duck, scared by sounds, fluttered away in a splash of wings.

Every time I lifted my head I could see that damned highway, the morning traffic cruising soundlessly in a shimmer of pink sun on windshields. Would I ever be able to surf here again?

"Mostly I surf at Trestles," I'd told Chloe. I remembered the way I'd tried to act cool, tried to impress her. Why had it seemed so important then? Nothing was important anymore. Did Chloe know yet? Maybe all the kids who'd been at the party knew, the phones ringing off the hooks. "Did you hear about Bry Harmon? Yeah, dead. No, his brother is OK. *He* jumped."

12

A wave lifted me and floated me gently up and over. "How far ahead would you say Bry was?"

I paddled for shore and waded out. Up under the lip of the sandbank, someone moved, stood. I knew who it was OK. Sowbug, our resident beach bum. He sleeps here a lot, curled up under a ratty gray blanket, hugging a big old jug of wine. Ours is one of Sowbug's three or four private beaches. Everything he owns is in a cardboard box that he stashes behind the big rock by the tunnel entrance when the police throw him into jail for a night or two. The kids get a kick out of playing tricks on old Sowbug. Once a bunch of them put rocks and stuff in his box while he was sleeping and busted a gut watching him stagger over and try to lift it. Another time when the Bug was sleeping, Pete Carboneri emptied out what was left in his jug and filled it with window cleaner. Sowbug would have swigged it down and never known the difference, but Alexander was there, and he grabbed the stuff and poured it into the sand with Sowbug trying to save it and hitting at Alex with his fists.   vasn't there, but somebody told me. I don't know if w   low cleaner would kill you or not. Sowbug seems to be   'e to drink just about anything.

The minute he saw me coming out of the water he began weaving toward me, waving his arms. "Hey, boy. Come here, boy." Sowbug always wants to talk. Old times, old politics dating back to the time he lived in Chicago, all of it muddled and senseless.

I never like talking to Sowbug. He turns me off and it's hard to be sorry for someone who's stoned all the time. I for sure felt no sympathy for him today. "Boy, wait up!" he yelled, but I pretended not to hear and went as fast as I could away from the tunnel area and up across the ice plant and the tufty grass to the highway. Over there was where it had happened. Jeez! Why was I doing this? Why was I looking like this? Was I morbid or something? On the other side, gleaming on the asphalt, was a small, dark stain. My heart began thumping. Not

13

blood. Why would I even think that was blood? There were blobs of tar and everything on this road. The police had had lights here last night and they'd taken photographs and measured the skid marks. They'd have noticed blood. But maybe they wouldn't have said.

I was running across, the weight of the board pulling me on one side, the highway hot already and sharp with pebbles. I stood looking down at the stain. Just oil. If it had been blood I'd have had to wipe it up. There was no way I could have left it.

A car came fast behind me and I scrambled sideways and leaped the way I'd leaped last night, sprawling in the long grass on top of my board. Another car whizzed by, and I stood and hefted my board through the wire that divides the highway from the ranch on the other side. The ranch is private property. Cattle graze here and sometimes you can see a real cowboy on a horse, his dog running beside him. The grass was full of prickles and hidden thistles where I crawled through, but I didn't care. The traffic was outside. In here I was safe.

I'd walked maybe fifty yards when I saw it. I was almost at the entrance to Del Mar, but if I hadn't been on this side of the wire I'd have missed it altogether. There are old beer cans and wine cooler bottles and Colonel Sanders chicken bones, black with ants. Lying beside an empty Doritos bag was a brown leather loafer.

Bry's shoe.

I picked it up. How did it get here, so far from where he'd been hit, from where he'd thumped onto the hood? Could it have sailed through the air like a thrown baseball, tumbling over and over to land here in the middle of the garbage? I was shaking and my stomach began to hurt. I stared across the wire at the highway and suddenly I knew. This was where the car had stopped. This was where those faint black skid marks ended. Somehow, Bry's shoe had come off on the hood, and whoever was driving had opened the window, reached out, and thrown the shoe over the wire. How could anyone *do* that? What

14

kind of monster? I stood looking down at the blur of brown leather, and I moved my fingers carefully so they held only the heel.

"Prints," I said out loud. "If we can find him we've got him, Bry. And I'll find him."

3

I COULDN'T CARRY the shoe home with me because Dad or Mom might see it, and I couldn't leave it lying there, either. I couldn't. If I'd had a backpack, or even pockets . . . But there was only my wet suit, sleek and tight and useless. At the gates into the park there's a little cubbyhole of a place where a guy sits and checks ID cards to make sure you live here and don't just use the parking area for the beach. It was too early for him to be on duty. I put Bry's shoe behind there, carefully out of sight of the entrance. It looked so lonely and abandoned I almost started bawling again. But there was something strong taking over inside of me now, an anger that eased my guilt at being alive while Bry was dead. Already I was finding anger a lot easier to handle.

The park was coming awake as I walked slowly between the rows of trailers. I saw Mrs. Daniloff, who lives in Number 1A, moving around inside her living room. She spotted me and came running out. "Jesse! Jesse!" Her arms were around me and I was breathing in her warmth and comfort along with the strong smell of bacon. She must have been cooking breakfast. "I'm so sorry about Bry,"

16

she whispered. "So sorry. Tell your mom I'll be up in a little while, and not to worry about what you're going to eat tonight. I'll bring a chicken casserole that will put you over for two or three days."

"Thanks," I mumbled. "I'll tell her."

It was strange. Everyone in the park knew already. Actually, it wasn't strange. We all know stuff about each other almost as soon as it happens. Somebody leaves his wife; somebody's pregnant; somebody's kid gets into college, we know. The park has its own instant grapevine.

I was stopped every few yards as I walked home.

"They'll get the bastard that did it, you'll see," the Captain told me. He wasn't wearing his braided captain's hat. I don't think I'd ever seen him without it and I hadn't realized his head was totally bald.

The Strathdee sisters brought out their little dog, Fluffy, and Ernestine said, "Fluffy says he liked Bry a lot. Fluffy says he hopes they catch the bad man who hit him." The sisters always talk through Fluffy.

I nodded. "Thanks, Fluffy."

Mom's right, I thought. The park people are wonderful. It is like being part of a big, caring family.

Later she and I drove to the airport to pick up Grandma and Grandpa and Aunt Lila, while Dad took the bus into town to make the mortuary and funeral arrangements. The Captain had volunteered to go with him, but Dad said thanks anyway, he thought he could manage on his own.

It's awful how many horrible business things you have to do when a person dies.

The plane from Minneapolis was late. They gave us some reason about bad weather at the other end, so Mom and I sat waiting. After a while I wandered out to the parking lot and walked up and down between the rows of cars, hoping. Not that I'd find the death car. That would be asking too much. But hoping I would see something that would jog my memory. I had a pen and I found a stub of a parking ticket on the ground and made myself some notes of things that might make one car different from another seen from

17

the back in the half-dark. There were cars in the lot with yellow diamond signs on their rear windows—BABY ON BOARD. There were a few bumper stickers, mostly with the kind of political statements you'd expect at John Wayne Airport in Orange County. I saw expensive-looking cars, all right, Mercedes and Cadillacs and BMWs. But none of them and nothing on them rang a bell. What *had* I seen last night? And if I couldn't remember now, what chance was there that I'd remember later? I sat on the wooden fence, staring blankly at the hot sheen of cars in front of me, thinking that the mind is a strange machine. I seemed to have shut off whatever I'd seen on that car, and yet I could remember so clearly the things about last night that I wanted to forget.

"Hey! You!" A guy in a security guard uniform was heading toward me. "Are you waiting for someone, young man?"

"Yeah. Well, I'm waiting for my mom. She's inside."

He pushed back his cap and squinted down at me. "Is your car in this lot?"

"No. Actually, we found a spot right at the front and . . ."

"I suggest you go inside then and wait with your mother. You've been walking around out here for quite a while now. Long enough, I'd say."

His eyes were the toughest I'd ever looked into. "OK. Well, sure. I'll just go on inside."

I backed away, feeling guilty for no reason whatsoever. Guilty and hopeless.

It was bad, bad, bad all over again when Gran and Grandpa and Aunt Lila came. "Fred's so sorry he couldn't get away," Aunt Lila told Mom. "He's devastated."

"It's all right, Lila. It doesn't matter."

Grandma hugged me tight and said my name over and over. Grandpa shook my hand. He had cut his face shaving and there was a smear of dried blood on his chin. He looked very old.

Grandpa and Bry have always been close. Ever since Bry

was little Grandpa has sent him stuff to make—plane models, and ship models when he was in elementary school, and more complicated things when he got older. Grandpa would get a model for himself at the same time, and they'd make them together, thousands of miles apart. Little notes came and went in the mail: discussions of their problems, the relative merits of glues, how B118 would not fit into C118, no way, not unless you trimmed it first, and Grandpa would definitely write to the manufacturer. They'd probably been working simultaneously on whatever that was on Bry's desk. I wished I'd swept all those bits and pieces of paper into the drawer before Grandpa could see them.

When we got home I did that fast. Then, while they were picking at the salad Mom and I'd fixed for lunch, I slipped away to get the shoe.

The beach swarmed with people and there were lots of cars parked along both sides of the road, the way it always is on Sundays. I studied them. White cars, silver, blue, most of them small. There was one big old dark green surfer wagon that looked homemade. I decided I'd probably be checking out the rear ends of cars as long as I lived, or till the day I found the right one, whichever came first.

Three kids on the beach side pointed across the highway. They'd be saying, "Over there's where it happened. It threw the guy right up in the air." Something like that. Kids are gruesome. Bry and I were. The mothers of those kids would have told them, "See? See what happened to that poor boy? Now maybe you'll know I'm not being paranoid when I tell you to stay off the road and use the tunnel. Don't ever, ever, ever again try running across the highway."

I swung around and that was when I saw the guy in the black Windbreaker. He was standing behind the ranch wire, looking at the spot where Bry had been hit, and the anger fizzed up inside me again. Not *his* brother. Not someone he loved. Just another geek.

"Hey!" I yelled. "What are you staring at?"

His hands jerked off the wire as if he'd been electrocuted.

"Why don't you step over and get a closer look?"

The guy turned quickly and began half running. Maybe I sounded like a madman. I felt like one, all right. There was some kind of emblem on the back of his black Windbreaker, a circle with airplane propellers or something inside. That's what I aimed for as I picked up a handful of pebbles and flung them at his retreating back. They missed by a mile.

"Have a good day!" I yelled. He was falling all over himself trying to get into his beige Honda, and I flung another handful of pebbles as it hurtled past me. It took a lot of deep breathing before my shaking stopped, before I could make myself move toward the back of the guard's office.

Chris Sanchez, who works the gates, was out checking the ID of someone coming into the park. I dropped the shoe into the brown paper sack I'd tucked inside my shirt. Already I'd decided not to put it with Bry's things. What if Mom saw it? Nobody that I knew of had questioned the missing shoe. There had been too many other things to worry about. Back home I put it on the shelf at the back of my closet, out of sight, and then I went to the phone in Mom and Dad's room and called the police. I held for Officer Valle, and when she came to the phone I told her in a low voice about the shoe, and about how I thought it had gotten onto ranch property.

"That's not a conclusion we can definitely make, Jesse," she said. "Not unless you saw it being thrown."

"I didn't see. I just know, that's all."

"We'd better get it over here right away in any case," she said. There was silence on the phone. "It's too bad you moved it," she added.

"If you ask *me*, it's too bad you missed it." I was angry again. "What did you expect me to do, leave it lying there?"

"That would probably have been best," she said mildly.

"I handled it carefully, don't worry. I hardly touched it at all. Do you think you can get prints off it?"

"It's possible."

"Well, look, I don't want you coming up here. I'll bring

20

it over," I said and hung up before she could object. It wasn't till then that it hit me. What if the guy in the black Windbreaker had been in there behind the wire looking for that shoe? What if he'd thrown it and realized afterward that there could be fingerprints there? I almost picked up the phone again to call Officer Valle back. But I just about knew what she'd say: "That's not a conclusion we can definitely make, Jesse." And she'd be right. I was grasping at straws.

Still, I wished I'd chased after him when he loped away toward his car. If there was anything I should have known, he'd have told me. Maybe I'd never lay eyes on him again.

But I did. Two days later at Bry's funeral. He was there.

4

My friend Alexander came down from Pasadena, where he's a student at Art Center. He'd signed up for summer school, and I'd known June, July, and August were going to be a bummer without him. Lonely, too. I hadn't known how lonely because I hadn't known I wouldn't have Bry either.

The funeral was to be at 12:00 noon on Tuesday. The days till then ran together in a blur of pain . . . of forgetting for a few minutes and then remembering, of sad conversations, of sympathy calls, of tears. There were a lot of "if only's." The "if only's" were almost the worst.

Monday night the family was in the living room, worn with suffering, talking quietly about the last details for tomorrow. Grandpa wasn't there, and I figured he might be outside on the deck in the sad, lonely dark. I thought about going out to see but decided not to. There were times now when each of us needed to be alone.

But when I went along the hallway to the bathroom, I saw a light from Bry's half-open door. Grandpa was sitting at Bry's desk. He'd found all the pieces of paper that I'd swept into the drawer and he was intently sticking one square of white cardboard to another.

"This is a tough sucker," he said to me, turning around and shaking his head. "But it won't beat us. Bry and I have licked things this tough before."

"Yeah." Someone had made the bed. I sat on the blue chenille cover Bry's had for ever and ever, and Grandpa turned back to the model. Tacked on the bulletin board above the desk was the cover of the model box with its picture of the finished product. CONSTRUCT YOUR OWN WORK- ING PAPER CLOCK, I read. 160 PIECES. HAVE A PRECISION ENGINEERED TIMEPIECE THAT ACTUALLY WORKS. So that's what it was. Pinned beside it was a cardboard sign. TIME HEALS. Underneath, in red marker, Bry had scribbled, "But not 100%." Right, Bryan. Sixteen years hadn't healed what those German measles had done to his ears. Not any percent.

"I like this stage," Grandpa said. "You can't believe you can ever take this kind of mess and turn it into something recognizable." He'd laid the pieces out in some kind of mixed-up order. There were paper cogwheels, ladderlike strips, circles with stars in them. That irritating memory flitted suddenly into my mind again. I picked up one of the circles and turned it between my fingers. Had there been a circle of some sort on the back of that car? But when I squeezed my eyes tight shut, trying and trying to bring it back, it turned into the circle on the back of that black Windbreaker the guy had worn. No good. No good at all.

"Do you know this girl?" Grandpa asked.

"Which girl?" I knew which girl.

"The one Bry was making the clock for."

"No. I mean, yes. It must have been for Chloe Eichler. I didn't know he was making a clock for her."

"She's a hearing girl, he told me. Bry was pleased about that. He said they were walking through Laguna one day, and she saw a beautiful old handmade clock in an antique store window that she wished she had for her room, and Bry decided he couldn't afford that, but he could sure make her a handtooled one." Grandpa turned, holding the two

23

rectangular ladder pieces, one in each hand. "Do you want to finish it for him? For her? I'm doing one at the same time at home. We could check up on each other."

I stood and smoothed the chenille cover, not looking at him.

"Well, I don't know. I don't have that much time. I've signed up for a really heavy load . . ."

Grandpa raised his eyebrows. "You have the summer."

"I have a job lined up for Taco Bell, but now I'm not sure. I'll think about the clock. But it doesn't seem right, Grandpa. This was his. For her."

"Of course it would be right. Who else is there?"

But Grandpa didn't know how I'd seen Chloe for the first time that night, how I'd been thinking about her right at the minute Bry was killed. How I'd been wishing she was my girl and not his. Those were the things that made it seem not right for me to be taking over where Bry left off. Those, and other things. "I think I'll go to bed," I said.

Grandpa sighed. "Yes. Tomorrow will be hard. But Jesse . . ."

I stopped.

"Take that job, Jesse. It's going to be harder for you if you don't keep busy these next months. You get to just lying around thinking, and that can be bad."

I nodded. "Good night, Grandpa."

I'd decided to stay alert during Bry's funeral, to check who was there and who wasn't. You never could tell. But it wasn't easy to stay alert. In the first place, this was my brother's funeral. That was *his* coffin placed in front of the pulpit, candles at either end, flowers piled high on the polished wood.

This was Bry's favorite hymn we were singing. In church he'd sing it with us, no tone and too loud most of the time, the way he'd talk too loud, not knowing he was doing it.

" 'Amazing grace, how sweet the sound,' " we sang. I was having trouble getting the words out. Why hadn't amazing grace saved him? Why hadn't he sensed that car, felt

24

the vibrations the way he could so often? For the same reason I hadn't heard it. It had been on us too fast.

I gave up trying to sing, standing still, letting the sound of the hymn wash over me, and I knew that my father wasn't singing either. My mother was, though, and when I looked up at her face I saw a sort of healing there. Maybe what I saw was amazing grace.

The church overflowed. All the park people had come. Just one of the Strathdee sisters, though. Even for a funeral Fluffy couldn't be left alone.

There was Chloe with her brother, and a man and a woman who were her parents, I guess, and Bry's shop teacher and Ms. Diprolini, who is the principal at the high school. A red glow from the good shepherd stained-glass window slanted across Chloe's face. She was wearing a dark blue shirt and skirt, and I thought, *Bry's girl*. His hearing girl. I hated myself for even looking at her.

Mr. Lichen, Bry's speech therapy teacher, my father, my grandfather, and I carried the coffin along the aisle after the service was over. Bry didn't feel heavy at all. When he used to jump on my back he'd felt heavy, all right, but not today. The aisle seemed awfully long, though, and the smell of the flowers sickening. I was glad to get outside into the air.

I don't think all the people who'd been in the church came to graveside. I would have liked to skip this one myself.

I looked at the clusters of people standing on the grass, a safe distance from the fresh mound of earth. There were faces I recognized and others I didn't. Most of the kids who'd been at the party that night were there, serious and pale now, not looking at each other or at me. Jim Lugar had come up to me outside the church as I waited to get into the limo, and he'd mumbled something about being sorry and he'd shaken my hand.

"Sure," I'd said, wanting to pull my hand away but not doing it. Senseless to blame him. Senseless to think that if

25

he hadn't passed out on the couch he'd have driven us home and Bry would still be alive.

Alexander was there, of course, with his mother and her boyfriend. I saw Officer Valle, too, and that surprised me because I didn't think a cop would get personally involved enough to go to a funeral. But then, what did I know?

She'd called back Sunday morning and said she was sending a cop car for the shoe, and I'd met it at the park gates and handed over the brown paper bag. "Don't go losing that," I'd told the driver. He looked about my age and his uniform seemed brand-new.

"I know what it is," he'd said in a bored, superior way.

I wondered if I should try to ask Officer Valle today about prints, but it didn't seem quite the time.

And that was when I saw the guy with the black Windbreaker again. He was standing at the back of the crowd, his hands in his pockets, his eyes fixed steadily on the Reverend Orville as he spoke the final words. Maybe the guy was just one of Bry's teachers that I didn't know? Or even a cop? But would a cop or a teacher have rushed away like that when I'd yelled and thrown that gravel? Maybe. I'd probably looked pretty spaced-out and hostile, no question.

I guess I was staring at him too intently because his head jerked suddenly in my direction and he took a step backward over a bump in the grass.

The Reverend Orville lifted his arms for the benediction and my mother and father and I held hands as we bent our heads. When it was over and I looked up, the guy had gone. Somewhere in the hushed silence a car motor started.

He'd run again. Why?

My grandmother leaned on Aunt Lila's arm. "Time to go, Jesse," she said. "But oh! It's hard to leave Bry behind."

"I know, Gran. Awfully hard." We walked together to where the limo waited and I kept telling Gran not to look back, but that was hard, too. Even as we stood by the car people lined up to hug us and whisper sympathy.

Officer Valle came and shook our hands. "We've had no word yet from the lab," she told me quietly. "I'll let you know."

I nodded.

"I'm very sorry about your brother," she said. "I've seen so many lives wasted, so much death, but I never get used to it. It's supposed to get easier, Jesse, with time."

"That's what they tell me. Time heals. By the way, did you notice the guy in the black Windbreaker?" I asked.

"I noticed him. I noticed everybody. I noticed when he left, too."

"I have a bad feeling about him. An instinct. But I guess bad feelings and instincts don't count for much in your business."

She adjusted the scarf at the neck of her jacket. "I wouldn't say that, Jesse." She nodded and was gone.

I knew Alexander was waiting to say something to me and I thought he was the person standing behind me. But when I turned, still half watching Officer Valle, it was Chloe.

"Hi, Jesse."

"Hi."

She put her hand on my arm. "I don't even know what to say. Bry was a great guy."

"Yes."

Her face twisted up. "Everything seems so . . . so inadequate. I wanted to yell and scream and . . . and just wail. You know, the way women do in some other countries, throwing themselves on the ground and howling? I think it would have helped. We're all so calm and civilized."

"I know. I keep thinking if I could find that driver . . ."

We stood, looking at each other, understanding.

"I've thought of something we could do," Chloe said. "We could make posters asking if anyone saw anything. The kind they do for missing kids."

"My grandfather and my father are offering a ten-thousand-dollar reward," I said and Chloe nodded. "Good. But we should do the posters, too. The more publicity the better. I've got stacks of markers and paints."

"You want us to work together?"

"I thought it would be a good idea."

"Well . . ." I didn't want to work with her, or see her again. I didn't want to finish the clock for her. Bry's girl. Hadn't I done enough to Bry? Hadn't I let that car hit him? I was looking over her head at the broad, smooth grass with its sunken-in copper plates and little bouquets of flowers. So neat. So tidy. You'd never believe this place was full of dead people.

"Look," Chloe said. "I'm going to do this anyway. I can get somebody else to help me. Any of Bry's friends would do it with me. I just figured since you're his brother, you'd want it to be you. No sweat. Forget it. I can handle it." The dark blue, dark-lashed eyes were definitely not friendly.

I could feel myself weakening. What harm could it do just to work on this with her? It was for Bry after all. "How many do you plan on making?" I asked.

"Twenty or so. I thought we'd put them up all the way from South Laguna to Corona Del Mar. Newport. We might even need more."

My mother was calling softly from the car. "Hello, Chloe, Thank you for coming." And then, "Jesse. We're waiting."

"You'll come?" Chloe asked. "Tomorrow?"

"What time?"

"Ten."

"My relatives don't leave till eleven."

"The afternoon then?"

"OK."

Well, I told myself as we drove away, I'd *tried* to get out of seeing her again.

5

THERE WASN'T ROOM in the car for all of us to go to the airport next morning, so Mom and Dad went. It was hard to say goodbye to Gran and Grandpa. Harder still to be alone in the trailer for the first time since Bry's death. I've been alone here hundreds of times. But the place was never this empty.

As soon as I'd washed up the breakfast dishes and set them to drain I was ready to get out of here. I checked the clock. In a couple of hours I'd be heading for Chloe's. For now I'd go up and say good-bye to Alexander. He'd be leaving this afternoon, and there was something I'd thought of that he could do.

The morning was gray and foggy the way it often is till the sun burns through around noon. I grabbed my red parka off the coat tree that stands by our front door and there, underneath, was Bry's old brown one. I stood, looking at it, feeling my throat close up, wondering if I should move it or leave it alone. No one had openly taken Bry's things from the living room, but they'd all disappeared. His beach walkers, which he usually kicked off under the chair. His new *Surfer* magazine. Grandma and Grandpa had given him a subscription for that and *Popular Mechanics* for Christmas. One of the little computer games he played and was so good at had mysteriously vanished from the coffee table. I suspected Aunt Lila. But she'd missed the jacket. I lifted it down and held it against my face, feeling the hurt come all over again. There was probably no end to this hurt.

In his room I slid open his closet door and hung up the jacket. The closet smelled of Bry, a mixture of old gym socks and the cologne I'd given him because it brought me out in a rash. His dirty-clothes basket was on the closet floor, full to overflowing. I looked at it for a minute and then set it outside the closet. I'd do these up in the laundry room with mine sometime. Not today, or tomorrow, or the next day, but sometime when I could handle it. I was just about to slide the door closed again when I saw the picture of Chloe inside, Scotch-taped to the wall. She was wearing a bright blue swimsuit, the kind that's cut higher than high on the sides. The picture was full length and she had one arm around a surfboard, its nose stuck in the sand. She was pushing back her wet black hair as she laughed at the camera. Surely her eyes weren't really that blue. It must have been a reflection of the swimsuit.

I closed the door and stood staring at the smooth, blank wood "Bry's girl," I said out loud to the empty room that had belonged to my dead brother.

I walked across to the desk. The paper clock pieces were organized in some kind of way. Stuck on the box front was a yellow-lined stickum sheet. On it, in Grandpa's writing, it said, "Jesse . . . let's get this finished."

"I don't think so, Grandpa," I said.

Outside, the Hegeman's cat, Stumpy, came to rub himself against my legs. I picked him up and carried him with me part of the way up the hill to Alexander's. There was some comfort in the warmth of him, the loud cat purrs.

The geraniums that grow wild on the sides of the park road sparkled with mist and spiders' webs. Beyond the wire, on the ranch property, two brown cows grazed. It all looked so peaceful, but I didn't feel any peace.

Alexander's mother greeted me with the pitying look I'd been getting from everyone since Bry was killed. I know they mean well, but I wish they'd quit it. If I smile bravely I feel fake. The only honest thing to do is burst into tears and that starts everything off all over again.

"Alexander's packing, Jesse," she said. "How's your mother?"

Everyone asks me that, too. They don't ask about Dad. I guess dads are supposed to be stronger or tougher or less caring, but it isn't true.

"They're both holding up pretty well," I said.

I told Alexander that I wanted him to make me a kind of police sketch and why, and he stopped packing right away and went to his drafting table. Alex has a real architect-type setup in his room, with a high stool and a clip-on lamp. Their trailer isn't as big as ours, but there is just Alex and his mom, and their two bedrooms are spacier than our three. Alexander wants to be a commerical artist and I guess he will be. He's good enough and creative enough, and he got into one of the best schools in the state. He pinned a sheet of drawing paper on the slanted desktop, sat on the stool, and said, "OK, Jesse. Talk to me."

"The guy had a kind of long face and a long chin. His hair was straight and about down to his collar. Dark brown. I think it was parted on the . . ." I closed my eyes, visualizing. "In the middle."

I waited while Alexander's pencil moved, the head and hair taking shape as if by magic.

"No, there were sideburns. I'm pretty sure. The squared-off kind."

Little by little we reconstructed the guy in the black jacket.

"Too bad you didn't see him in the churchyard." I smudged the sideburns with my thumb to make them spread out more.

"I wasn't looking at anybody in the churchyard," Alexander said quietly. "Are these eyes right?"

"They're good. But the nose should be longer, pointier." When we were finished Alex held the drawing at arm's length. "What do you think?"

"I think anybody who knew him would recognize him, that's for sure."

Alexander rolled the drawing and snapped a rubber band around it. "Where are you going to ask about him?"

"Everywhere I can think of. Chloe and I are going to ... I mean, Chloe said she and I should ..." I stopped. Why was her name so hard for me to say? Why was Alexander looking at me so carefully?

"You're talking about Chloe Eichler?"

"Yes. She was a friend of Bry's. We're putting up posters. I thought I could show this at the same time and ask if anyone knows him."

"Isn't that almost libel?" Alexander lined up his colored pins along the top of his board.

"I won't be suggesting anything. I'll just ..."

"Better not show the picture in the same places, Jesse. That might make it guilt by association."

I stared at him. "Who are you? Melvin Belli?"

Alexander grinned. "No, I just watch 'Moonlighting.' " He spun around on the stool. "Want to go walk on the beach? I won't be home again for a while."

I stole a quick glance at the clock. Still time, before Chloe's. Then I stole a quick glance at Alexander. Did my face change when I thought her name? If it did, he hadn't noticed.

It was still damp and gray outside. On the way past our trailer I ran in and left the drawing on my bed. My parents weren't home yet. The plane for Minnesota was probably late again. I pictured the five of them standing around the airport, worn out, with nothing left to say except a few last "if only's."

I closed the trailer door behind me and ran to where Alexander waited.

The beach tunnel was dank and musty. I kept my eyes down, watching my feet scuff along so I wouldn't have to see those happy, white-painted names on the wall.

"You know, the chances of that guy being the hit-and-run driver are infinitesimal," Alexander said.

"I know. But infinitesimal is better than nothing. Right?" I'd told Alexander about the shoe. "If I can find him, if I can get his prints somehow, if the police can get prints off the shoe, if they match." I heard all those "ifs." "Anyway, it's worth a try," I said. "He's all I've got."

Someone was calling, the old voice cracking and high-pitched, "Boys! Boys!"

"Sowbug," Alexander said. "What in heck has he done to himself?"

Sowbug came staggering over the sand, disturbing a gathering of cold-looking gulls and sandpipers. Somebody had done a heavy job of makeup on his face, probably when he was stretched out on the sand, dead asleep. His lips were slick red, eyeliner ringed his eyes like a raccoon's, his eyelids were bright green, a lopsided scarlet spot glowed on each cheek. On his upper lip a black, curling mustache had been painted over the gray stubble.

"You boys got any money?" Sowbug scratched at his arms under the torn red sleeves of his flannel shirt.

"What do you need, Bug?" Alexander fished in his jeans pockets. Alexander is always nice to Sowbug. Nicer than I am.

"A five?" Sowbug asked hopefully, and Alexander laughed. "Are you kidding? I've got seventy-five cents and that's it."

Sowbug's hand shot out and grabbed the silver.

"You got any, sonny?" He blinked up at me out of his red-rimmed, black-ringed, bleary eyes.

"I got nothing." I patted my pockets to show I meant it. And even if I had, I decided, I wouldn't have given it to him. I'd given before. We all have, from time to time. But now I felt like snatching Alexander's seventy-five cents back. For more booze? That's what he'd buy. We treated

33

Sowbug OK. He was somebody to tolerate and be cool about. A bunch of us had even hidden him once under a bundle of towels and sat on him while the beach patrol was checking. We'd saved him from a for sure three days in the lockup. No more. I was through with drunks. Even non-driving drunks.

Sowbug held a trembly hand to his face. "Say, ain't you . . . Ain't it your brother . . . ?" Still mumbling, he began staggering backward.

"God!" I said. "Even Sowbug knows."

"Bug," Alexander called. "You'd better wash off your face if you're going up to Safeway to spend that cash, or you're going to get a lot of attention."

Sowbug was still walking backward, holding his hands out in front of him as if to ward us off. "I didn't see nothin' and I don't know nothin," he said in his shaky whine of a voice.

My heart began to race. "Wait! Sowbug!"

He had turned and was shuffling toward the tunnel as fast as he could, but I caught him in a few strides.

"You were sleeping here that night, weren't you, Sowbug? The night my brother was killed?"

"Naw, I wasn't."

"You were here. You're always here."

"No, I'm not." He stared at me with indignation. "I got a place. A place of my own. I don't sleep here. It's against the law."

"Please, Sowbug," I said. "Please, if you saw something tell me. Nobody's going to bust you for being here. I promise." I had a grip on his arm. It was like holding a stick that would snap if I squeezed.

"How could I see anything? I told you. I wasn't here." I guess I was squeezing too hard now. "C'mon, boy," he whined. "Let go of me."

"What did you see?"

He pulled against me and I was shaking him, not hard, but maybe it would have gotten hard if Alexander hadn't grabbed me and pried my fingers off.

34

"Are you crazy, Jesse? What are you hurting the old guy for? He doesn't know anything."

I was panting as if I'd run a marathon. "He was here."

"So what if he was. He can't even see what goes on under his nose. Just relax, Jesse, will you?"

I rubbed my hand across my eyes. "Listen, Sowbug." Such a reasonable, ordinary voice. "I'm sorry if I hurt you. But you have to talk to me or the police because I'm going to tell them."

"No. Don't do that, boy. They'll take me in again."

The morning after Bry was killed Sowbug had run toward me. Right here, on this beach. Maybe he'd just wanted somebody to blab to, or maybe he'd seen something and wanted to spill it. If only I'd stopped and listened. Now he'd had time to think it over and he'd decided to keep quiet. That way he'd stay out of trouble. Or maybe he had truly forgotten. I ought to understand about forgetting. Sowbug couldn't have that many brain cells left in one piece.

"I swear it on my mother's head. I didn't see anything." He inched away from me, and this time I didn't go after him. He'd be back.

6

I WALKED TO Chloe's, staying well into the grass on the side of the highway, Alexander's drawing tucked inside my shirt.

I recognized Chloe's mother from the funeral when she opened the door. Mrs. Eichler is a typical-looking, well-to-do Laguna mother, unlike mine who has short gray-and-black hair and wears T-shirts that say SAVE THE WHALES. Chloe's mother has stiff golden hair and a face as pretty and smooth as a candy egg. She was wearing spiky high heels with dark gray slacks and a dark gray, silky sort of shirt. I noticed she even had a chain with a diamond in it around one ankle. An ankle chain!

"You're poor Bry's brother." Her smile was tight and careful. "We were so sorry to hear about the accident. Please come in."

"Thanks." There was a nervous wariness about her. She probably wasn't sure of how I'd be after what had happened. I couldn't blame her. Minute to minute I wasn't sure myself.

The hallway and living room were certainly different today. No kids on the couches or making out in the corners.

36

No empty glasses on the piano. No smells of beer and burning joints.

"Chloe told me what the two of you are doing. It sounds like a practical idea." She waved toward the stairs. "Her room is the second on the right."

I vaulted the steps two at a time, wondering if Chloe hadn't heard the bell. I'd thought she'd be the one to open . . . Part way up, I stopped. What did I think this was? A date for the prom? An ordinary boy-girl visit?

Her door had a silly-looking little ceramic plate with the words CHLOE'S ROOM and a border of blue flowers. At least I knew I was in the right place. I knocked, ran my hands through my hair, and waited till she called, "Come in."

I tried not to stare. Wouldn't you think a girl would have a tidy room? This place was worse than mine. Two surfboards lay in a corner. A wet suit was draped across the dresser mirror. I guess that was a dresser underneath, though it was so jumbled with stuff that it was hard to tell. There were fins and rubber boots and a surfleash and a weight set with weights stacked any old way. The room had a pink carpet, pink frilly curtains, and a bed with a pink canopy that had clothes tossed on top of it and the end of a fishing pole sticking out like an antenna. Probably it was a really nice room, stunning, as the decorating commercials on TV would say. This one was stunning, all right. But in the wrong way. There were more things hanging on the wall than would hang in any junk shop—even an old Halloween skeleton. I thought of Bry's clock. Where would it go?

Chloe lay on her stomach on the pink rug facing a lifesize poster of Sting that tilted at a crazy angle. She was surrounded by marker pens and discarded sheets of white paper.

"Hi!" She looked up. "I think I've finally gotten it right."

"Hi," I said. "You shouldn't have bothered picking the place up just because I was coming."

"You noticed. My mom notices, too. She's given up. When I was little she used to tell me that a lady lays out at night what she'll wear in the morning. She's sorry she ever said that. I lay out a year ahead. And a year behind. If there's one thing I don't want to be, it's perfect. Perfect is suspect. Anyway, Jesse, tell me what you think of this."

I squatted down beside her, pulling out the picture and setting it on the floor between us. She held up the poster. I read:

DID YOU SEE WHAT HAPPENED ON COAST HIGHWAY
AT APPROXIMATELY 11:30 PM ON JUNE 20?
A SIXTEEN-YEAR-OLD BOY WAS HIT AND KILLED
BY A CAR THAT DIDN'T STOP.

The blunt, no-nonsense words made me feel suddenly sick and I closed my eyes.

"Oh, Jesse! I'm sorry." Chloe scrambled up. "How awful to push it at you like that! I'm such a clod." She ran her hands through her hair. "It's just . . . if we do this . . . it won't make his death unhappen, but . . .''

"I know." I cleared my throat and stood, too. "Maybe we could be more specific, though. Coast Highway covers a lot of territory. Could we say 'across from Del Mar Beach'? And don't forget the phone number." I was trying to be logical and practical and all those good things.

"Sure. Perfect idea." I sensed her relief that I wasn't going to throw a conniption fit.

She lay down again on her stomach, her legs scissoring behind her. Her shorts were khaki-colored and her shirt matched. She looked as if she were going on a jungle trip to shoot lions. I took a deep breath and realized that the room smelled better than mine. It smelled of girl.

I knelt beside her as she penciled in the extra words. "You don't think a picture of Bry . . . ?" she asked.

"No. I don't think a picture would help anyone. Either someone saw, or no one did." Immediately Sowbug popped into my head.

Chloe slanted me a blue, anxious glance. "You'd *think* anybody who saw would call the police. But then, why are we bothering to make posters? We've got to believe that someone saw, but didn't know *what* they saw. They didn't know how serious.''

I'd been there. I'd seen and forgotten. All I'd kept was something round and white . . .

Something *round* and *white*? A circle? I jumped up, walked toward the window, and stared into the branches of a tree, grasping at the white circle that was already slipping away.

''Are you OK, Jesse?''

''Yeah.'' *Don't go, damn it! Don't go, white circle!*

I sat on the edge of a chair that was piled with a mountain of stuff and put my head in my hands.

Chloe touched my shoulder. ''Would you like to just give this up for now, Jesse? We can do it another day.''

''No. I'm OK.'' I stood shakily, got the drawing, and unrolled it. The guy stared out at me, the paper curling top and bottom. ''Do you know him, Chloe?''

She shook her head. ''No, but he looks familiar. Could be I've seen him around. I don't remember where. Why?''

''He was at Bry's funeral.''

''So were a lot of people.''

''I know.'' I rolled the paper up again.

''We could ask Wilson when he gets back next week,'' Chloe suggested. ''He knows everyone. Right now he's camping up in Washington with Lugar and some other guys. 'Course, he may not get back next week. Wilson isn't exactly into hanging around home.''

I batted the sketch against my leg. ''Let's make more posters.''

Chloe worked on the floor, and I cleared a space for myself on her desk. Slow jazz played on her stereo, and outside, birds called to each other in the trees. I could hear skateboard wheels on the sidewalk and kids' voices. ''Hey, I can do a gorilla jump.'' ''Cannot. That's not a gorilla jump.'' ''Is too.''

We'd each finished six posters when her mother came in with a tray of lemonade and chocolate-chip cookies. I couldn't help thinking how innocent parents are. Lemonade

39

and cookies! Mrs. Eichler would have freaked if she'd seen what was being consumed here last Saturday night. Chloe sat yoga fashion on the floor, bare brown legs folded like petals.

"Did you know my brother was making you a clock?" I asked abruptly.

"A clock for me? Bry?"

"Yes. A wall-hanging one. Of paper."

Chloe put the cookie she was eating back on the plate.

"I guess you admired a clock once, when you were with him."

"I remember."

A fly had gotten into the room somehow and buzzed around her glass.

"And he was making one for me? God, he was such a nice guy!"

I thought I'd never seen anything as gentle as her face. She looked like an angel. The way she looked made my throat hurt.

"How complicated, though, to make a clock," she said at last.

"I think he liked doing it. I think he would have liked doing anything for you."

"Oh." She gave me a hard-to-interpret glance and picked up a marker. "I suppose we'd better finish these posters." *Not to change the subject or anything*, I thought.

We did twenty before we stopped again.

"Should we go right away and put them up?" Chloe asked. "We could take my car."

Of course she'd have a car, like all rich high-school girls.

"Great," I said. "The sooner the better."

Their two-space carport was empty. Her dad's and Wilson's wheels were gone, I decided. The garage held a white Ford Galaxie and a white Mustang. Not anything black or dark. There was no way I could help checking Chloe and her mother along with everyone else.

"I guess the Mustang's your's," I said.

"Yes. Dad bought it for my birthday. I wanted a

40

Bronco." I can't get my boards to fit in this, but Dad says Broncos are unfeminine. He and Mom are very into me being feminine."

"I don't think they need worry too much," I said.

She leaned across from the driver's side to open the passenger door for me. "You don't think they need to worry about what? Not getting my boards to fit?"

"No, about you not being feminine." The minute I'd said the words I wanted them back. They seemed too flip for someone whose brother had just been killed, especially since this was his brother's girl. "Did you and Bry go driving a lot?" I wished those words back, too. What was my problem here? And why did I sound so damned surly?

She edged the little car out into the sunshine. "Not much." Her voice was as cool as mine.

We drove toward Laguna, the ocean on our right, sparkling blue at the ends of the streets that spiraled down to it. On our left the houses perched like white gulls on the dry brown hills.

"I think Bry and I went driving twice, though I'm not sure why you want to know. Once I took him to the surf shop at Dana Point, and once I drove him to an appointment with his speech therapist. Your mom was supposed to drive him but something went wrong with your car. Bry asked me. And I said OK."

"Oh. Well, thanks for taking him."

"You don't have to thank me. Bry did that a long time ago." We were stopped at a red light and her fingers drummed on the wheel. She didn't once look in my direction.

We pinned the first poster up in the U-DO-IT Laundromat in the mini-mall. It was a dank, tacky place, empty of everything except chipped machines and abandoned socks and fluff balls that scurried like mice across the concrete floor. The poster looked so new and clean in the muddle of old carnival notices and ads for pizza to go. That poster was one of the saddest things I'd ever seen. I wanted to tear it off. But that would be stupid. There was no one in

41

there to show the picture to, but I tried every place else we stopped. No one knew the guy in the black Windbreaker.

At the Razzle-Dazzle Video Arcade the manager came out from behind his glass door as soon as we appeared. "Would it be OK if we put this up?" I asked, showing him the poster.

He read it once, then again, his lips moving, before he handed it back. "Sorry, man. No way. I don't want no notices like that in here. Too big of a bummer. This is a happy place. A fun place." He scissored his arms back and forth across his chest to show me no way, nohow, never.

"Thanks," I said. "I can see that kids' welfare means a whole lot to you. You get them in here every day and . . ." I stopped. He wasn't looking at me; he was looking at Chloe, swaying back and forth, his hands in the pockets of his red blazer.

"Hey! You're the looker who was in here that time with the deaf kid. The one who racked up all the numbers? Man, was that bozo a whiz, or what? I never saw a more coordinated kid, and him as deaf as a dish."

Chloe fluttered one of the posters. "This *was* the deaf kid. He's the one that got killed."

"Oh, wow! Hey, I'm sorry about that." The guy rubbed his chin. "That's this kid here? Look, I'll find a place for a poster, you can count on it."

Chloe handed him one, but I plucked it back from his hand. "Don't bother. We don't need one in here."

I could hear Chloe saying something to him as I walked away, then I heard her running to catch up with me. "Don't be so pigheaded, Jesse. Jillions of people come in and out of here."

I slowed and looked over my shoulder. The manager was still staring after us.

"It's for Bry, Jesse."

I turned. "I'd appreciate it if you would put this up," I said. And then, "I'm sorry I blew my stack. He was my brother, OK?"

He took the poster I held out. "OK, man. No sweat."

Chloe and I were back in the car. "It was the way he called him the deaf kid," I said, rolling down the window, letting air at my hot face. "As if he were some kind of freak."

"He was a deaf kid," Chloe said. "A really smart, nice, good-at-everything deaf kid. Look . . ." She had the key in the ignition but she didn't turn it. "I know everything's real rough for you right now, Jesse. But are you always this difficult? I mean, even with me. I was a friend of Bry's. I hurt, too. But sometimes you act as if you hate me, or resent me, or don't want me around. If you don't want me butting in, just say so."

"No. I want you."

She started the car. "I'll take you straight home, OK?"

"That will be fine. And thanks a lot for everything you did. I appreciate it. The posters, the driving, everything."

"You're welcome. I did it for Bry."

She let me off at the park gates and I watched as she swung the little car around and eased it out into the flow of traffic. Across the highway the night sea glimmered like silver. Headlights came up and over the hill in a steady double stream, turning into a double stream of scarlet tail-lights as they passed. Chloe had gone. I'd probably never see her again. And probably that was best.

7

MOM HAD TO drive Dad to work next morning. I went, too, and we swung around and stopped off at the cemetery first.

"The police went door to door in the park yesterday," Dad said as we walked up the curving narrow path that led between the grave markers. "They were there while we were at the airport. I guess they asked questions of everyone. Joe Grossman told me." Joe Grossman is the park's maintenance man.

"Mary Daniloff said they went through the tunnel and talked to the lifeguards," Mom said. I wondered if they'd talked to Sowbug, too.

It was another gray, foggy morning, mist falling like white rain on the headstones. Bry didn't have one yet. Dad had ordered it from Crocker Brothers but it would take a while. For now there was just the brown earth, the wreaths of flowers beaded with fog and already turning brown.

My mother shivered, looking across the churchyard to the band of colorless ocean. "I wonder if the sun's shining inland? On a morning like this I feel like moving from the beach. It's so damned dismal.'' She wrapped the edges of her long coat more closely around her.

"On a morning like this I feel old,'' my father said, turning away for the long walk back to the car.

He looked old as he walked into the big glass-and-concrete building in Irvine where he works as one of the electricians. How could he have gotten as old as my grandfather this quickly?

It was almost nine when we got home, and I was about to go down to look for Sowbug when our doorbell rang. Officer Valle and Officer McMeeken stood outside. Behind them, ghostlike, was their Laguna police car.

"Is there something new?'' my mother asked. "Has something turned up?''

"I'm afraid not.''

"Oh,'' Mom said in a flat voice. "Come in anyway. Would you like some coffee? I just made a pot.''

"No, thanks, Mrs. Harmon.'' Officer Valle was wearing a big scarf, white-and-beige stripes over a big, bulky sweater. I wondered if she kept her gun under that sweater or in her purse. She unwound the scarf and smiled across at me. "How's it going, Jesse?''

"OK, I guess.''

"Did you happen to remember anything more about that car?'' Officer McMeeken pulled what was probably the same notebook out of his parka pocket.

"Not really. And I've been driving myself nuts trying.''

"I know how that can be, in the middle of the night . . .'' Officer Valle smiled that nice smile. I tried to imagine what she would have been like at my age. All those little scars would have been pimples then. She'd probably been self-conscious as hell. But not anymore.

"I have a suggestion, Jesse. How would it be if we go back down there, on the highway, and re-enact what happened?''

My mother made a little sound and Officer McMeeken turned quickly toward her. "We'll have all the traffic

45

stopped, ma'am. There'd be no danger to Jesse, I promise you.''

"How do you feel about it, Jesse? Can you handle it?" Officer Valle asked.

"I suppose. If you think it'll do any good.''

"No guarantees. But let's try." She wound her scarf back around her throat. "And ma'am?" She stopped in front of my mother. "I hope it won't inconvenience you too much if someone from our lab comes by to get some fingerprints from the trailer here.''

My mother's hands fluttered to her throat. "Prints from here? Why?''

"Oh, it's just routine. The police department's full of fomalities.''

Mom looked at me for support.

"It'll be all right, Mom." I thought I knew why they wanted those prints.

I drove with the two officers through the park.

"Did you get prints off Bry's shoe?" I asked.

"There are some on there all right. They're smudged, though. Some seem to be your brother's. Some will be yours and probably your mom's. We'll have to see what's left.''

I didn't want to ask when they got Bry's—or how. I knew anyway.

Officer McMeeken put out red flares to block off the north-bound traffic, and Officer Valle asked, "Ready, Jesse?''

I nodded and began walking where I'd walked on Saturday night. It was different now. Day instead of night. There were no cars behind me. That same smoky flare smell, though, that had been there afterward. Traffic coming toward Laguna slowed to a crawl to gawk, and I heard Officer McMeeken shouting, "Come on. Move it along. There's nothing to see.''

I kept walking. On Saturday night Bry had been here, in front of me. He'd been alive then. Dead now, under the dead flowers. I clenched my fists in the pockets of my denim jacket and tried not to start bawling. *You're here to remember*, I told myself. *Remember, dummy!*

I didn't hear the police car cruise up behind me till its lights came on and its brakes squealed, and I dived onto the side of the road just the way I'd done then. This time, though I didn't call out first. There was no one to call to.

The car skidded to a stop where the other one had stopped. I lay, bawling for sure now, biting the back of my hand, staring at its rear bumper, the brake lights, the trunk, the back window. Nothing.

Officer Valle was beside me. "It's OK. It's OK, Jesse."

"I don't remember a damn thing," I whispered, banging my fist against the ground. "They were round and they were white, that's all I know."

"They? More than one?"

I nodded slowly. "Two. White circles on black."

"How big Jesse?"

"Big as . . . big as the top of a jar. And something, some shape inside the circles."

"Anything else?" Her voice was quiet and easy.

"No."

I stood and began pulling bits of wet grass off my jeans and she helped, neither of us talking. The cop car backed up and Officer Valle left me and went to kick the flares to the side and stamp them out. We got into the car and she patted my shoulder.

"See? It's coming, Jesse, bit by bit. It will all come."

"I was wondering about hypnosis. Maybe I could try that and I'd remember everything."

"Hypnosis is tricky. In the first place, it's questionable in court. It would be better if you'd remember naturally, Jesse. And I believe you will."

Chris Sanchez waved from his post on the gates as we went past, and Officer McMeeken half turned from the driver's seat. "Did anybody question that kid in the booth?"

"He goes off at nine P.M. so he was gone before it happened. Too bad for us." Officer Valle handed me a

47

Kleenex from her big, black purse. I'd thought she hadn't noticed that I was sniffling a bit.

"Did you talk to Sowbug?" I looked out the back window at the beach, at the empty sand and three brown pelicans flying low across the cold sea. "You know who I mean?"

"The old fellow who lives on the beach? We know him well. He wasn't there yesterday. Probably gone on vacation to another beach for a few days, up to Scotsman's or down to Aliso. Or somewhere with a tunnel. Sowbug likes tunnels he can crawl into."

We were stopped now in front of our trailer and I could see Mom, pale as a shadow behind the window.

"I think he was there that night and he may have seen something." I waved reassuringly in Mom's direction. "But he's paranoid about going to jail."

Officer McMeeken grinned at me in the rearview mirror. "And we treat him so good, too. Free bed and board."

"He won't talk to *you*, that's for sure," Officer Valle told him. "You tease him too much and he doesn't understand. Old guys like Sowbug spend their lives scared of cops. Will he talk to you, Jesse?"

"He wouldn't. But I'm going to try again." I opened the door.

"Jesse? Tell your father Channel 5 has agreed to run his reward notice tonight as a public service. We could get something from that."

"I'll tell him."

Mom had made more fresh coffee and we sat at the table and drank it and ate wheat toast, and I told her what had happened and that nothing had happened, and we each pretended to read the *Bay News*, rustling the pages as if this were just another morning. Except that normally I wouldn't be here; I'd be up in Westwood. And normally Bry would. I turned a page. There was a swimsuit ad for one of the expensive stores in South Coast Plaza. A girl, on a beach at sunset, wearing a dark swimsuit, seriously studying a shell that shone pale and transparent. She was beautiful. Her hair was short and black like Chloe's, and she was all

48

shining legs and hollowed shoulders. I'd make a bet her eyes were blue. I made myself turn the page again.

"Isn't it ironic," Mom said loudly. "I don't drink, your dad never has more than a couple of beers, and here's our son, killed by a driver who was probably drunk." She was hidden behind the paper, which shivered in her hands. "Doesn't that seem ironic?"

I got up and stood behind her and kissed the top of her head.

"Sh, Mom. Sh."

There were going to be lots of mornings like this.

After we'd cleared up she said she thought she'd go to the Safeway. They had a special on canned tuna, three for a dollar. It's hard to believe sometimes how the mind can slip from death to canned tuna. It must be some kind of release valve. I said fine, I had laundry to do, and she asked if I'd take the bathroom towels and wash them, too.

We always have lots of laundry quarters in the yellow ceramic pig on the dresser. As soon as she left, I dropped a handful in my pocket, stuffed my clothes and Bry's and the towels in the big laundry bag, and left, too.

Our laundry room is at the top of the hill on the high green, with maybe the best ocean view in the whole park from its two dirty little windows. Bad architectural planning, somehow. The only saving grace is that the gazebo's there and it gets the view, too. I slung the bag over my shoulder and began hiking.

The sun was coming through the gray sky now, and the gazanias in the borders in front of the trailers were beginning to open their yellow and orange eyes. The park gazanias are like the park people: They stay closed up till the sun appears.

Miss Ernestine and Miss Gabby and Fluffy were in the laundry room. I don't like doing the wash when they're there. They're so modest about their things, standing in front of the folding tables, shielding the privacy of their laundry with their bodies. I'm almost afraid to glance in the

49

direction of the tumbling clothes in one of their dryers in case they think I'm a Peeping Tom.

"Good morning," I said, and rubbed Fluffy's head. He had gook in the sides of his eyes. I don't think I've ever seen Fluffy's eyes when they weren't gooky, but the sisters don't seem to notice.

"Fluffy's so happy to see the sun," Miss Gabby said, "I think I'll just take him out on the grass for a few minutes, Ernestine."

"Do. Certainly." Miss Ernestine kept her head bent while I filled two washers and stuffed my clothes and the towels in one, Bry's in another. For some reason it seemed important to keep Bry's separate.

"I think I'll go outside myself, Miss Ernestine," I said. "You won't let any thief rip off my wet laundry while I'm gone."

"No, indeed, Jesse." She had a pink spot on each cheekbone. Poor Miss Ernestine has a hard time talking to me when things are normal, and these days they for sure aren't normal. I was mooching toward the door when her little, high voice stopped me.

"Jesse? I have something to say to you."

I turned and I was getting that strange, creepy feeling again. Miss Ernestine *knew* something.

I sat down, keeping an empty chair between us. Any false move and I felt she'd run, run out to Miss Gabby and Fluffy and safety.

She turned a box of fabric softener in her hands. "We didn't tell the police when they came to our door because it probably is silly, as Gabby says, but . . ." She took a deep breath and shot a glance at the window where Fluffy was sniffing at the oleander hedge and where Miss Gabby stood beside the gazebo looking down on the million-dollar ocean view.

"The night your brother was hit by the car, Gabby and I took Fluffy for his evening walk. We always watch 'Spenser for Hire' at ten on Saturday nights. Spenser is such a gentleman! Then we walk Fluffy to the gate so he can . . . you know . . ." The pink spots deepened.

"Sure, I understand. And you walked down Saturday night. Is 'Spenser' an hour show?"

"Yes. So at about ten after eleven, or maybe a quarter past, because we had to put on our coats and get Fluffy's leash and lock up and . . . and that's too early, you see, because your poor brother, poor Bry, was hit at eleven-thirty. Isn't that what the paper said? And besides, the car was going the wrong way."

I guess I was staring at her too hard. She gave a little nervous jump and began pulling ribbons of softener from the box, shredding them. "It is silly to have mentioned it after all, isn't it?"

"No. It's not silly. You mean you saw a car—a car that you noticed for some reason—but it was going south, toward Laguna. It wasn't coming from Laguna?"

"That's right. And the reason we noticed it was because the driver was weaving all over the highway. Gabby said to me, 'Ernestine, would you look at that car!' And there it was, coming round the curve. It went up on the grass, almost off the cliff. I thought for a minute it would go over, and then it swung across, right at us, Jesse. We picked Fluffy up pretty fast, I can tell you." She was trying to cram the ribbons of fabric softener back in the box. " 'That driver is *drunk*, Fluffy,' Gabby said."

"Could you tell me what the car looked like? What color it was? Big? Small? Anything?"

"That just the trouble. Gabby and Fluffy and I have gone over and over it. It was a dark car. We know that for sure. But I think it was dark green and Gabby thinks black. It wasn't small, the way the Sanchez boy's is small, but it wasn't as big as the Captain's."

Chris Sanchez drives a VW bug. The Captain has an old Cadillac.

"About medium then." My heart had started that same, heavy thumping. "Did you see the driver, Miss Ernestine? Was it a man?"

51

"Oh, my, we didn't stay around long enough to see anything like that. There were these big headlights, dazzling, coming right at us and you can't know..." She stopped and began tearing at the fabric softener again. I knew she'd remembered that, yes, I did know what it was like to have great dazzling lights coming at you, back or front. "We just picked Fluffy up and retreated, Jesse. Retreated."

"I don't blame you. You didn't see anything on the back of the car after it passed? Some round things maybe? White? On the bumper or rear window?" I was struggling for words, for that memory again, but nothing more would come.

"I *did* look back over my shoulder. That car was going up the hill still on the wrong side. If another car had been coming..." She paused. "I hope I didn't simply muddy the waters telling you this. That's what Gabby said we'd do. And besides..."

"Besides what?" I prompted.

"It couldn't be the same car that killed poor Bry, could it, Jesse?"

"I don't know." There was nothing to say a car couldn't go south, make a turn around, and come back north. What were the odds against two cars, within a half hour of each other, on the same highway, both with drivers so drunk that they were out of control? I tried to be realistic. On a Saturday night, with parties and summer starting and weekenders and vacationers? Come on, Jesse. There could have been a dozen drunk drivers passing Del Mar. But in a medium-sized, dark car? Yes, in a medium-sized, dark car.

"Oh, and Jesse, it was sort of rounded. I mean, not squared off at the back." Her hand made a curve.

I nodded. "Yes."

I could add another fact to my memory now. The car that hit Bry had been rounded at the back, too.

8

I WENT SURFING just after dawn next morning. And it was a little better than the last time, when I'd given up and crossed over the highway and found the shoe. "It's supposed to get easier," Officer Valle had said. Probably. But it would never be easy.

I'd walked the beach before I'd headed for the water, looking for Sowbug, but he wasn't there. He'd be back. Even though Sowbug does sometimes disappear, he always comes back.

It was a pretty morning, without our usual overcast. I rode a few waves, letting the beauty and the loneliness comfort me a little, and then I sat between the pearliness of sea and sky and tried to think. If a car came toward Laguna at 11:10 or 11:15, spent five or ten minutes somewhere, came back at 11:30, where could it have gone? What was within that distance and time radius? All-night markets, liquor stores, gas stations. Friends who lived in the area. Maybe just a stop to have one more for the road. To drink another beer, do another line of coke, turn, blaze back along Coast Highway, and smash and kill.

A swell was coming and I let myself slide off my board into the cold clean sting of it, going under, coming up. Did it matter if the car came that way first? I didn't know.

I paddled for shore, stashed my board, and walked the highway again, on the beach side, facing the traffic. This was where the Strathdee sisters had seen the car rounding the curve. "It went up on the grass, almost off the cliff," Miss Ernestine had said.

Cars aren't allowed to park here on the bend. Farther on, there's a break and an area that used to be an old riding stable and horse trail where you can pull over. But here the traffic breezes by, not daring to stop. Cars breezed past me already, even this early.

I stopped partway around the curve. Up on the soft edge, dangerously close to the drop, was a tire track with a deep indented pattern. I stared at it, knowing it might be a match for the ones the police had found where Bry was killed, thinking it might be important. I wished there was some way to rope it off, but there wasn't. Nothing to do but get my board and haul it and me home as fast as I could.

My parents were up. I heard my father in the shower and the small sounds of my mother in their room. She always tidies up and makes the bed before she comes out to fix breakfast. Chloe's room would drive her nuts.

It wasn't seven yet but I dialed the police station and left a message for Officer Valle to call me. She did later, while Mom was driving Dad to work, and I told her about my conversation with Miss Ernestine and about the tire marks.

"Maybe it isn't major," I finished. "But I thought you should know."

On the phone I could hear the babble of voices, other phones ringing, a clicking that might have been typewriter keys. I imagined the station house the way it is on TV, with prisoners being brought in and sleepy cops going on and off duty.

"Everything's major, Jesse," Officer Valle said. "We'll get someone from the lab out there right away."

"Let me know," I said.

* * *

She called me back on it early the next week. The tracks were the same. "I should tell you we found more in the sand at Clambake Point. It seems logical to suppose the car came south, cut in at Sapphire Cove Road, turned at the Point, and came back, heading north again. And the only people who know you can get to the Point along that road are the locals, right?"

"Right," I said. "And the surfers. And kids from school who go there to make out or do drugs or booze."

I pressed the cool earpiece of the phone against my forehead, figuring out the time. It fitted. Too bad he hadn't driven himself off the edge instead.

"Is it logical to suppose he was stinking drunk?" I asked.

"We don't know that, but it's certainly a possibility."

"It's certainly a possibility," I mouthed soundlessly back at the phone. These cops were so full of it!

"Jesse?" Her voice was tiny and tinny through the phone. "We're keeping at it, Jesse. We'll find him."

"Sure." But when? And how?

It was a terrible week. We had phone calls on the reward and on our posters, and I found out that people can be greedy and cruel and ghoulish and that they lie a lot. I found out, too, that people can be caring, and sad for you, and kind. We had cards sent to us, and religious poetry. Strangers told us we were in their hearts and prayers, that masses were being said for Bry, that candles were being lit. A businessman in Newport added another five thousand dollars to Dad's reward money. A scout troop collected eighty-three dollars, and a psychic whose name was Madame Zara told the police she saw the car plainly and it was a hearse with pale curtains and a casket inside.

Officer McMeeken said, "At least she didn't say it was being pulled by six black horses," and then he coughed and looked uncomfortable.

Alexander invited me to come to Pasadena for a while, but I told him I had too much to do. I spent a lot of time at Clambake Point or up in the gazebo or drifting aimlessly

55

on my surfboard. I made endless lists of what I knew and what I didn't. Three or four times I convinced myself that I should call Chloe and tell her what kind of response we'd had to the posters. I even got out the phone book to look up her number. It wasn't hard to find. On the E-for-Eichler page one name was underlined in yellow Day-Glo pen. I didn't call her and I didn't write the number down, but it kept repeating itself over and over inside my stupid head. How could something as unimportant as a phone number stick, and those missing details about the car drop into nothingness?

On Thursday Crocker Brothers told us Bry's headstone was ready and they'd be erecting it, so we went out to the graveyard that evening and stood in the long red rays of the sun and read the simple words that told who lay there, under the earth. Mom had brought honeysuckle from the hedge by our trailer and when she put it in the vase of water a ladybug flew out from the tangle of yellow. A Del Mar ladybug. I wished it would stay there, with Bry.

Friday afternoon, because I had to do something, I took the bus into Costa Mesa. The fireworks stands for tomorrow were doing a rush last-minute business on the edge of town. Little kids and their parents crowded the counters, getting their sparklers and spinning jennys. One of the best things about living at the beach is being able to shoot your Fourth of July firecrackers into the ocean. It's illegal now, but the kids still do it anyway. Bry always liked the cherry bombs best, even though he couldn't hear them.

"It's fun to see people's faces when those suckers explode," he'd say.

Not this year, Bry. No Fourth of July for you. "No sun, no moon, no morn, no noon." Miss Sharp's English literature class. Great memory, Jesse. Selective.

I got off the bus in the middle of town and walked around the car dealers, looking at what they had in their lots, and then going inside to pick up their advertising. Once in a while a hotshot salesman would come over. Probably thought I was some kid with mega-rich parents who were about to buy me a postgraduation gift. Or a birthday gift. I flashed onto Chloe and her little Mustang.

"Did you and Bry go driving a lot?" I'd asked.

Mom wasn't home when I got back with my plastic bag full of junk. The evening paper still lay on the path of the trailer door, and when I picked it up I saw that the reward notice about Bry was in again, upped to fifteen thousand dollars now. I wanted to hide it so Mom wouldn't have to look at it when she got home, or Dad either. But there was no place to hide from any of this.

I sorted through the leaflets I'd picked up, dumped those that had the big luxury cars or the small economy models, and spread the rest on the table. Camaros, Thunderbirds, Buicks. I was looking for a rounded back, even white circles. There were too many damned cars. Soon I couldn't tell one from another. Soon I knew I wasn't going to find what I was looking for.

Tomorrow was the surfing competition finals at White Sands. My mind kept slipping to that. Chloe would be there. Thousands of people would be there. Maybe the guy in the black Windbreaker. Maybe the death car.

I got up and went into Bry's room. Neither Mom nor Dad had touched anything yet. When would they be able to? Maybe never. The pieces of the paper clock were still neatly stacked the way Grandpa had left them. I picked up one and put it down again but I didn't slide across the closet door to look at Chloe's picture.

"I think I'm going to the White Sands competition tomorrow," I said abruptly, after dinner.

Dad pushed up his glasses and rubbed his eyes. "Good idea. You should get away a bit, Jesse. We won't need the car, Mother, will we? You can take it, Jesse."

"Thanks. I thought I'd just ask around, see if anybody saw something or heard something, you know." There was definitely this need in me to make an excuse. What right had I to be going to a blast of a surf competition when just two weeks ago my brother had been killed? What right had I to be hoping to see his girl?

9

WHEN I GOT to White Sands at eight next morning, the
parking area was full. I found a space way at the back,
locked everything up tight, and zigzagged across the lot,
up one line of cars and down the next. Every make in the
world seemed to be here. I checked bumper stickers, parking
permits, logos. There were rainbow decals, dice that hung
in rear windows, religious emblems. It's ridiculous what
people hang and stick on their cars. It was ridiculous that
I couldn't remember what was hung or stuck on that one.
I gave up and headed for the beach.

No stadium could be as perfect as the one for a surf
contest. I looked across the sloping silver sand of the bleach-
ers, at the grandstand that was the pier. Already they were
filled with bodies, huddled under sweats and blankets, waiting for the action to start and the day to heat up.

I moved to the far end of the crowd, inspecting each row,
each cluster of spectators, but if he was there I didn't see
him. Then I pushed through to the steps leading to the pier
and walked behind the mob, all the way to the bait shop
and the fast food stand on the end. I didn't see him. I didn't

see Chloe, either. But of course I wasn't looking for her.

There was a space on the pier on the second row and I squeezed myself in. Big, official-looking White Sands Pro banners had been tacked up at intervals, and spectators had made their own posters for Tom Curren, World Champ and local surfer, and for Terry Richardson, who's older and has been around for a while, and who's always a favorite.

I was wishing I'd brought binocs so I could see the faces of the people sitting on the beach, when I spotted Chloe. I'm not sure how I recognized her. She was on the sand, about a hundred yards down from the pier, sitting in a folding chair. Maybe it was her red, hooded sweat shirt that made her stand out. Maybe it was the yellow towel she'd tucked around her legs. Probably got shorts on under there, I thought. Probably cold. I'd never have seen her if it hadn't been for that red-and-yellow combination. Or maybe I'd have seen her anyway.

OK, Harmon. Now you know where she is. Now forget her.

"Jesse?"

I turned.

It was Debbie Green, who'd been at high school with me. Junior high, too, for that matter. "Hi, Deb."

She flung her arms around me in a giant hug. "God, I was sorry to hear about your brother." Her face was squeezed against mine and I could smell something good, perfume or soap. "He was such a nice guy."

We held each other at arm's length, smiling shakily, and then she said, "Well, you're here and that's major. I can't wait to see Tom Curren ride those waves! Anybody got the pew in front of you?"

"It's yours." I wedged her in.

Debbie is blond with cute frizzy hair and the kind of skin that looks polished. She's tall and I had to peer around her head instead of over it. She and I have never dated, but I think we might have last year if we hadn't both been seeing somebody else at the time.

After a minute she turned around. "I saw one of your

posters. Betsy Forgreave and I were in the mall and it was in the Sports Hut window.''

"Oh, good." We hadn't taken one to the Sports Hut. Chloe must have made more. This time she'd left me out of it.

"Betsy said she'd seen a couple of others and we both caught the notice in the papers. Any luck?"

I shook my head. "Not yet."

"I hope you get some good leads, Jess."

"Yeah. Me, too."

The sun appeared and on the beach and along the pier sweat shirts and T-shirts were peeling off. I glanced casually toward the bright flag of the yellow towel and panicked when I didn't see it. I'd lost her now, lost her in the crowd. But then I saw the red sweat shirt, saw her bend over as if talking to someone on the sand beside her. Who was it? Was it a guy?

Out on the water things were beginning to happen.

"First heats!" Debbie threw me back a smile and at that minute the announcer's voice came loud and clear through the speakers, welcoming us, and a roar went up from the crowd.

Bry would have loved this, I thought. He'd have been here, probably sitting with Chloe, and I'd have been with them, because it would have been OK to have been with her if he was there, too. It wouldn't be OK now.

I asked a woman in front if I could borrow her binocs for a couple of minutes and when she handed them over I checked the crowd again, sweeping the glasses the length of the beach and back. I didn't think the guy I was looking for was here.

Each time the glasses swung toward Chloe I let them linger for just a second before I pulled them away. Strange, sort of sneaky, spying on her like this. She gave a great, wide yawn and stretched. I could see the smooth line of her throat and my own was suddenly dry. What was the matter with me? So she was a cute girl. The beach was full of cute girls. The one standing in front of me, leaning against me,

61

was a cute girl. Why didn't my throat go dry for her?

Out on the surf Dan McClure was going for it, showing us his backhand on a hollow left break. The crowd roared its appreciation, but I was having trouble getting into it.

By noon, when the quarterfinals got under way, the sun was blazing hot. Debbie had stripped down to white shorts and a bikini top, and I'd shucked my sweat shirt and tee and tied them around my waist. When I borrowed the glasses again I saw that Chloe had discarded her warm-up top and was wearing a silky red bikini.

"See all right?" Debbie asked, moving her head to the side.

"Yeah. I can see."

Deb held our places while I got us hot dogs and drinks, and after we'd wolfed them down I told her I thought I'd go check out the beach and did she want to come?

"No way," she said. "I'm not giving up this spot. You come back, huh? Don't miss the semis."

Last year at the semis a dog swam out into the waves, barking its head off, and a bunch of us plowed in after it. Bry had grabbed it first. Last year.

I told Debbie I'd for sure be back and took off. MTV was carrying the contest live and there were cameras and wires everywhere. The day was full of the smells of suntan oil and summer bodies, the exact kind of day my brother would have loved.

Not everybody on the beach was that interested in the surfing contest. There were people milling around far back in the sand, tossing footballs or just cruising, looking for happenings. Some of them were setting off firecrackers. A knot of guys stood in what might have been a football huddle and I had just passed them when I heard, from somewhere in the middle of the huddle, a girl's quick scream.

"No," she yelled. "Quit it, will you?"

Heads turned and the lifeguard scrambled down his ladder, heading for the group, which had grown somehow, and there were arms flailing and something was tossed out on the sand, grabbed up, and tossed in again. A red bikini top!

Chloe's? I felt sick. Couldn't be. Not Chloe's!

Now *I* was yelling, hurling myself against the outside bodies. "Let me in. Let her go!" I was clawing at heads and shoulders when somebody grabbed me. "Cool it, man! What's your problem? The girl's OK. Nothing happened to her. She crawled out. There she is."

I jumped so I could see over the heads, and I saw a girl with a white towel wrapped around her top, brown skin between the towel and her red bikini bottoms. She was at the side, laughing, covering her mouth with her hand. Not Chloe. Definitely not Chloe.

The guy who had talked to me grinned. "Thought she was your sister, huh?" I didn't have the strength to grin back. "They were just messing around. She was sunning on her stomach without her top, and they were telling her to roll over and take the rest off. Nothin' serious." He had blue zinc on his nose to match his blue surfer Jams. "But now she's not even there and they're fightin' like maniacs. It's getting more serious by the minute."

I took a deep breath. Not Chloe. I'd have punched out every single one of them if it had been Chloe. I was panting and covered with sweat. Where *was* she anyway?

The TV people sensed a story and were juggling their equipment across the beach, and the lifeguard was trying to push his way through the mob, which swayed back and forth, oozing in all directions, growing even as I looked at it.

A beer bottle was thrown, and then a beach chair, then all was chaos. The pier was emptying fast. People rushed like ants, spilling down onto the sand. A beach umbrella sailed like a parachute, and a firecracker ricocheted between the running legs. I heard the beat of the police helicopter.

Police cars roared up, but somebody on the beach had flares, the kind they put on the road the night Bry was killed, and they were lighting them and tossing them into the crowd.

"Oh, my God!" The guy in the Jams pointed to smoke in the parking lot and I saw a police car burning.

Where was Chloe? I pushed against the traffic of running bodies, heading for where I'd seen her last.

She wasn't there. Had I expected her to sit through this?

Two surfers still rode the waves and the announcer still talked. But he wasn't describing the surfing. "Ladies and gentlemen, please stay in your seats. You came to watch the all-pro finals. Please stay in your seats."

I ran along the edge of the surf among the abandoned chairs and towels and coolers, calling Chloe's name.

And then I heard her. "Jesse! Jesse, over here."

She lay on the sand on her side, and some guy knelt beside her. "She's hurt her foot pretty bad," he said. "I was just about to go for help."

"It's OK," I said. "I'll take care of her."

"So stupid!" She held up her foot. "Look!"

I saw the bright blood dripping, the gash about an inch long.

"Glass," she said. "I didn't think I should walk. Not in the sand." Her face under her tan was gray.

I unknotted my T-shirt from my waist and tied it on her foot. I don't like blood and I could see it beginning to soak through the pale blue cotton already. My stomach got that fast, empty feeling. My stomach's always the first thing to go anyway. I concentrated on Chloe. "I thought it was you in the middle of the mob. I thought they'd pulled off your top. I was trying to get in. I'd have killed them, I swear." I stopped, aware of what I'd been saying and how ferociously I'd been saying it. "Do you think you can stand if I help you?"

She pulled herself up, holding onto my arm. "You thought I was in there? And you tried to save me? Oh, Jesse!" Her face had that tender, angelic look again. But this time it was for me. It made me feel strange. That was her Bry look.

"It might be better if I carried you," I said.

She had a big, white canvas purse that banged against me as I lifted her. "What about your other things? Didn't you have a chair?"

"Forget everything. Let's just get out of here."

The parking lot was a milling mass of people and police and smoke. I staggered up through the soft sand. Guys carry girls easily on TV and in the movies. They must fake it. This wasn't easy at all. Chloe was heavy. My arms got tired and she'd slip lower and lower and I'd have to keep hiking her up. "I'll hop. Just put me down," she said about a million times. I puffed and blew like a big, old whale.

At the far edge of the parking lot I circled round the back. Once I glanced down at her foot and wished I hadn't. Black smoke drifted lazily around us but down closer to the beach it was thick and dense, billowing into the blue of the sky, hiding the palm trees and the roof of the restrooms.

"How could something like this happen?" Chloe asked. "It was going so well. Everybody was having such a good time."

"Who knows? Some loonies. That's all it takes." Never in all my life had I been so glad to see Dad's car. "Can you stand for a second, Chloe? Hold onto the roof."

I found the keys, unlocked the door, helped her to get in. The outside of the car was coated with a fine, gray ash and the inside was blistering. The seat must have been killer hot when she slid onto it, but she didn't say anything. I gunned the motor and backed out.

"Hang in there," I said.

"Will my car be all right?" she asked.

I looked across at her tight, hurting face and down to where the bloodsoaked T-shirt rested on the black rubber mat. "Let's worry about you now and your car later," I said. "And what happened to the people you were with anyway? Why didn't they stay with you?"

"They ran up to see what was going on. I told them not to, and I sat in my chair like a good little girl." She fingered wearily through her hair. "And then some firecrackers jumped in my direction. I got up, and I didn't see the glass."

Traffic was jammed at the exit and I had to stop.

"Was he here, Jesse?" Chloe asked.

"Who?"

"The guy in the black jacket. I figured he's the one you came to look for. I figured otherwise you'd never have come."

"Right." I edged the car in front of a van that almost took my ear off with the blast from its air horn. I'd forgotten about the guy in the black jacket. I'd carried Chloe through the sand and it hadn't been easy, but every second I'd been conscious of her hair against my check, of the feel of her skin, of the way I could see the pale swelling where the top of her swimsuit had moved. In all of that I'd forgotten him. And I'd forgotten Bry.

"I don't think he was there," I said at last.

"I don't think so either. Jim had binocs. I kept checking people out. I saw you," she added, "on the pier."

I had a sudden flash of Chloe watching me while I watched her. Crazy!

"I hope you didn't have to abandon the girl you were with because of me," she said, in a cool, casual way.

"No. I wasn't really with her. We met by accident." But I *had* abandoned Debbie. I'd told her I'd be back and I'd forgotten her, too.

Chloe shifted and groaned. More than anything I wanted to take her hand and comfort her. But I couldn't. At least we were moving now, picking up speed.

I was just as glad to see the hospital as I'd been to see Dad's car. I helped Chloe out, fished her sweat shirt from the big, white bag, held her as she struggled to get her arms into the sleeves. Printed across the front were the words CALIFORNIA, WHERE LIFE'S A BEACH. It didn't quite come to the top of the bikini pants. I put my own sweat shirt on, too, so I'd look a little more respectable.

They took us right away in the emergency room, though there were people ahead of us.

"Bleeders first," the nurse said cheerily. "What happened here anyway? Were you at that riot on the beach?" She brought over a wheelchair and eased Chloe into it. "Bunch of rowdies, those surfers," she said.

66

"It wasn't the surfers." I touched Chloe's hand. "Are you OK? Does it hurt a lot?"

"Not too much. And Jesse—thanks."

"Do you want me to come with you?" I asked.

The nurse butted in. "Are you her husband? Her father? Maybe you're her grandfather?" This nurse had wiggly eyebrows and a sense of humor.

"No."

"Sorry. Boyfriends don't count around here."

Chloe's eyes met mine.

"I'm actually not her boyfriend either," I said. "She's actually . . . she's . . . she was my brother's girl."

"Oh. *Was?*" The eyebrows wiggled again and the nurse grinned and swung Chloe's chair in a sort of wheelie. "She won't be long. You can wait."

I waited.

10

CHLOE HAD THREE stitches in her foot, a pad, and strapping. She carried my bloody T-shirt in a plastic bag.

I eased her into the back of the car, and she sat with her leg along the seat. That's probably where she should have been on the way in.

The Fourth of July traffic was bumper-to-bumper on Coast Highway, with pedestrians on the crosswalks and straggling across the street headed for an afternoon on the beach.

I spoke over my shoulder. "Does it hurt a lot?"

"Some. The doctor gave me a prescription for painkillers if I need them."

We were stopped at a light in the center of town right across from Main Beach Park with its picnic tables and swings. Guys leaped and jumped, smashing a ball back and forth across the volleyball net. They could all have been in suntan lotion commercials. Spectators jammed the tables and benches.

"One thing about Laguna Beach," I began, "there's always something going on." And then I saw it: the new restaurant that had opened on the bluff overlooking the beach. For some reason restaurants up there don't do well. They're too expensive, maybe because the rent's so high. This one had a new black glass sign, riding high on wooden stilts. THE WINDMILL. There was an etching, a white windmill on the black glass. I stared at it, seeing the back of the guy's black jacket. Not airplane propellors after all.

Behind us a car honked impatiently.

"He works there," I said softly.

"Who? Where?" Chloe struggled to lean across the front seat.

I pointed. "The restaurant."

"Jesse! I bet you're right. Pull around. See if he's there."

"I can't. That's a one-way street. And I've got to get you home."

"You do not. I'm OK."

"Your foot!"

"The heck with my foot. If you could only find somewhere to park."

There wasn't anywhere, of course. Not within a five-mile radius of the center of Laguna, not on the Fourth of July.

The blaring behind me was an angry chorus that stretched back and up the hill.

"Move it, man! Get that crate out of here!" In the rearview mirror I saw a bunch of girls in a convertible. *Blam! Blam!* That was one of them leaning on the horn.

"Hold on!" I told Chloe, and swung the car into a space by the curb clearly marked red for no parking.

"Chloe? Honest now, can you handle it for a couple of minutes while I check the Windmill? You see, if I find him it'll start getting easier. It won't bring Bry back, but I'm going to feel so . . . so vindicated!"

"Go, Jesse!"

I got out and ran back, past the summertime shops, pushing through tourists with their mounded ice-cream cones, throwing "sorry's" and "excuse me's" to right and left as I jostled toddlers and parents, jumping the sprawled bodies in the park. Jeez! Was I crazy? I'd be lucky if they didn't

69

impound Dad's car and take Chloe to the slammer. Nobody parks on red in Laguna Beach.

The narrow path up the bluff was bright with geraniums and purple ice plant. I ran till my heart hurt. The parking lot was filled with cars now. I stopped suddenly when I saw him, leaning against the rear brick wall, smoking a cigarette. He was wearing the black nylon jacket, black pants, and white tennis shoes. On duty in the parking lot. No wonder he hadn't been at the surfing contest! He'd been working.

He spotted me when I was about fifty feet away and heading toward him. Immediately he dropped the cigarette and began running.

"Hold it right there," I yelled, but he cut around me and galloped down the path with big, hungry strides. He ran diagonally across the grass.

The volleyball game had stopped. I sensed the sudden interest as I raced after him, still yelling. A girl was making giant soap bubbles with some kind of wire loop thing. I knocked over her bucket of detergent, saw for a second her startled, angry face.

He was in the soft sand now, weaving between the sun-bathers, bumbling through a little kid's sand castle, heading on down to where the tall apartment buildings front the beach. I wasn't gaining on him. The wooden steps here are private and most of them have a gate. He'd spotted an open one and he was racing up the steps, three at a time. He'd be out on the sidewalk then, in the crowds. He could dodge into one of the shops and be gone and I'd have lost him again. Unless he went back to the Windmill. He wouldn't, though; he'd be gone. A dog came barking excitedly at my heels, slowing me more. I was at the bottom step; he was halfway up.

If the woman hadn't decided at that second to come out of her apartment and start down to soak up a few rays I'd have lost him for sure.

She was a big woman in a yellow sundress and she carried a beach chair and a fringed umbrella. She blocked the steps all the way across and when he tried to push past her there wasn't an inch to spare unless she chose to turn sideways for him. She didn't. "What's going on here?" she demanded. "These steps are private. Are you a tenant?"

The guy tried again to shove her aside, but it was like pushing past Mount Rushmore. He turned, looked at me, at the few steps that divided us, then leaped over the stair railing into the bank of ice plant and sand below. I heard the thud as he landed one half second before I jumped on top of him. We lay there, the wind knocked out of both of us. It felt as if the struggle had been knocked out of him, too.

Above us the woman hung over the wooden bar. "I've a good mind to go back to my apartment and call the police. We don't need this kind of hooliganism."

"It's all right," I called. "Nothing to worry about."

I got the guy's arm twisted behind him as he lay on his stomach. He didn't resist.

She came down the rest of the steps, muttering as she struggled through the soft sand. I moved then so I was straddling his back, still keeping my tight grip on his forearm. No way was I going to lose him now.

"It's not a bad idea to call the police," I said, "unless you'd rather talk to me."

"I'll talk to you," he said. "And you can let go of me. I'm not going anyplace. Sooner or later I knew you were going to find me."

I still held him, though, as he staggered up, wriggling his arm and shoulder, stomping his right foot on the sand. There was something beaten about him. But I kept alert anyway.

"You killed my brother, didn't you?" Unbelievable how even and reasonable my voice was. I could have been talking about the weather.

"I don't know." His breath smelled foul. Old, stale beer and tobacco.

"You don't *know*?" I dragged him across to the bottom step and pushed him down. "Sit! How can you not *know*?"

71

"I just can't remember, man. I might have. I don't know."

"You wouldn't forget a thing like that! God, we're talking here about my brother's *life*." My cool was going fast and my voice was beginning to shake. I leaned over and grabbed the guy's shoulder. "You did it, you turkey! You killed him. You were drinking and . . ." I was shaking him so hard that his neck jerked forward and back, like a rag doll's.

"Quit it, will you? I was there. I admit it. But I don't know if I killed him. That's what I'm trying to say."

I stopped shaking him and stared down. "What do you mean?"

"I . . ." He spread his hands. "I don't suppose you have a cigarette."

"No. And never mind about a cigarette. Start at the beginning, the beginning of the night Bry was killed."

"I was working, parking cars. I got off at eleven. I went down to the Marina and I had a bottle of bourbon and a six pack in my trunk and I sat in my car and had a few and . . ." He looked up, shaking back his long, straight hair. The sand clotted in it sprayed out like water. "Look, could I just go down to those guys and see if I can bum a cigarette?" He jerked a thumb toward a group of surfers.

"No. keep talking."

"I guess . . . I guess I drove home, after. My car was outside in the morning. I'd parked it in the middle of the road." He tried a small laugh. "Good thing I woke early. four A.M." He leaned over and I tensed, but he just pulled a piece of ice plant and began shredding it between his fingers. "I had to push it out of the street. Dead battery. I'd left the lights on." His voice trailed away. "Then I read about your brother. That's the way I would have come home." He glanced up at me, then back at the ice plant. "I went to the place where it happened . . . where they said it happened. You know. You saw me. But I couldn't remember anything. If I did it, I'd have remembered back there, wouldn't I?" He was pleading with me, but I was the last person in the world he should have asked for understanding.

"Do you remember throwing his shoe?"

He cowered back a little. I guess I sounded fierce all right. "His shoe? I never saw no shoe."

He had the skinniest neck and I wanted to get my fingers around it. I shoved my hands in my pockets.

"The thing is," he said, "once before I found a big dent in my fender in the morning and I couldn't remember how I got it. And another time I was home and I had no car and I didn't know where I'd left it. That's why, you know . . ."

"But you don't quit drinking, do you? You don't quit driving?"

He didn't answer, trying instead to snap his ice plant stem, which bent like rubber. In the silence we could hear kids yelling in the surf. A sand crab scuttled under the bottom step.

"Where's your car now?" I asked. "Do you remember that much?"

"Sure. It's up in the lot, in employee parking."

"Let's go."

We climbed the forbidden steps. Fourth of July flags drooped from the lamp posts that lined the sidewalk. A guy on stilts, dressed as Uncle Sam, offered us a leaflet. Farther along I could see the front of Dad's car and I wondered if Chloe was OK. But I couldn't let myself worry about her now. The streets that lead to the beach are short and narrow. We turned down one of them, Broadway, and cut across the sand. The guy was limping bad but I didn't slow my pace.

"What's your name?" I asked.

He hesitated.

"You might as well tell me," I said. "You'll never get away from me again."

"It's Plum," he said. "Joseph Plum."

I nodded. We climbed the path between the geraniums. He was fishing keys and a handful of loose change from the pocket of his pants, heading for a beige Honda in the

73

corner of the lot. It was the same car I'd seen him get into that morning. He walked around the front and laid a hand on the hood. "See? No dents, no dings, nothing. That made me feel better, you know, when I read about the kid. I mean . . ."

"You mean my brother."

"These little foreign jobs, they bust a gut if you even look at them. If I'd hit somebody . . ."

"You could have had it in a body shop since then."

"No. I swear. And what body shop do you know that would do a job this good on a car this old?"

I stood at the back. It wasn't rounded. There was nothing round and white.

"Did you take something off of here? A decal? A sticker?"

He looked puzzled. "No, man! Nothing."

I bent down to look at the tires. They were almost bald. No way could these have left those deep marked tracks. The car was the wrong color. The wrong size. The wrong shape. It was the wrong car.

"Maybe you borrowed a customer's car to go drinking at the Marina."

"Uh-uh. Two other guys work with me. I couldn't get away with that. Besides, I remember driving there. In my own car. Getting out the bottle. I keep one under a blanket."

"Great," I said. "Good going."

He fumbled with his keys, carefully not looking at me.

"It wasn't you," I said.

"It wasn't?" His face was slack, the jaw hanging open. "You know that for sure? I mean, God!" The eyes had no understanding.

"I'm telling you, it wasn't you," I said again.

He leaned his arms on the hood and bent across them, head down. His shoulders heaved.

"Not this time, you punk," I said, and turned away before I'd give in to the temptation to smash his head down on the hard metal. "You'd better get help, buddy," I said over my shoulder. "You're death waiting to happen."

In the window of the Honda I saw my distorted reflection, my cold, angry-eyed face. Maybe I needed help myself.

11

I took Chloe home.

"So that's it," I told her when I finished my report about Plum. "Zilch."

"How can you be so sure?"

"I'm sure. Now I've got nothing . . . except . . ." I didn't want to, couldn't bear to explain about the shoe, so I rushed on, "And whatever stupid thing is buried in my head and won't come out."

I heard her shift a little in the seat. "Don't lose hope, Jesse."

I'd never liked my name, Jesse. When I was little I thought it sounded like a girl. But I liked it now, the way she said it.

"Yeah, well. And there's still Sowbug."

We drove in silence.

"It's weird, Chloe," I said. "I'm beginning to feel kind of sorry for Plum. He cried. I was so mad at the time . . . but now, knowing he didn't do it . . ."

"Don't feel sorry for him," Chloe said fiercely. "He could stop with this drinking and driving. There are places that his family and friends have probably been begging him to go to get help. He doesn't want to, that's all. Don't give me this poor-guy stuff. Bry's dead. You wouldn't be feeling this big about that creep if he had killed Bry.''

"You're right," I said.

"You bet I'm right. The creep!"

My father keeps a box of Kleenex in back; I heard the soft rustle as she pulled one out. In the mirror I saw her rub her eyes then rest her head against the back of the seat. "I hate liquor." She sounded tired all of a sudden. "I swear, I hate it more than anything. It destroys and destroys."

"Don't think about it anymore now," I said quietly. "Try to rest. I'm sorry you had to wait for me so long."

"Don't worry. A meter man came, though. I showed him my foot and told him there was nowhere for you to park and that I needed pain pills, which was certainly no lie."

"Chloe! I shouldn't have left you. I'll find a drugstore right now and get . . ."

"Uh-uh. I just want to be home."

I squirmed through the traffic, making as much safe time as I could. At her house I left her in the car while I ran up and rang the bell. It was her mother who opened the door. She was all dressed up in something silvery and she smiled her tight careful smile and said, "Hello, there," then looked past me. "Is that Chloe? Oh, no! What happened?"

"She hurt her foot but we've been to the emergency room and it's OK." I was having a horrible flash of déjà vu. Me, coming to another door like this, the cops with me, and Dad asking, "What's wrong? Where's Bry? Has something happened to him?"

Chloe's mother was running down the steps to the driveway, calling back, "Harry. Come quickly. Chloe's hurt," and I was running after her, but more slowly, my mind filled with the memory of my father's face that awful night.

"Don't get crazy, Mom." Chloe stood, holding on to the door of Dad's car, and now her father was running past me. He wore a white dinner jacket and black pants.

I stood back while the two of them helped Chloe up the

77

steps. Mrs. Eichler had on some sort of glittery stockings and her diamond ankle chain threw off its little sparks of light.

As soon as they got Chloe settled on the couch, I offered to go out again and get her prescription, but her dad said they'd phone it in and have it delivered right away. I guess that's the way super-rich people operate. He thanked me for bringing her home and asked if I'd had to help pay for anything in the emergency room.

Chloe said, "No, I had my credit card. Don't worry, Dad. You'll be getting the bill."

A good thing, too, I thought. The ten bucks in my wallet wouldn't have helped pay for much.

It took Chloe a few minutes to remember her car, and when I offered to drive her dad back to pick it up he said he'd appreciate that and it would be a good idea to do it quickly, given the situation over at the beach.

"We'll cancel the dinner party at the club," he told Mrs. Eichler. "The others will understand."

"I don't need you to stay home because of me," Chloe said quickly. "I've just got a cut foot. I'm not dying."

"Weren't you supposed to be going out with someone, too, tonight?" her mom asked.

"I can call. It was no big deal."

I wondered who the someone was. I wondered why I felt as if I'd been punched in the chest.

"You and Dad go to your dinner party," Chloe said. "All I want to do is go to bed anyway."

Her parents looked at each other. "We *could* find out if Josie could come over," her mom began.

"Oh, for heaven's sake, Mom . . ."

"I'll stay." Had I said that? I must have because they were all looking at me. And I had a quick sure feeling her mother didn't want me to stay. Probably afraid of leaving me alone in her house with her daughter. Date rape. Maybe I should back off, but I didn't want to.

Chloe shook her head. "You don't have to stay, Jesse. I've been enough trouble all day."

78

"No, you haven't. And I have no plans. This isn't exactly your every year, typical Fourth of July for my family."

The silence told me they remembered why.

"So if you're in a hurry, sir, I'll take you to get Chloe's car now and come right back."

"Great! I really appreciate it, Jesse."

"Me, too," Chloe said softly. I was stupidly glad that she appreciated it.

Her father tried hard to make conversation with me as we drove. About UCLA and my plans for the future. "A business degree is just about the smartest thing you can get right now," he said. "Then you can decide which way you want to go."

He said my car was in really nice shape and I explained that it was my Dad's and that he took good care of it. He told me he liked old cars, and he had an ancient Volvo himself that was his pride and joy. Probably not old and ordinary like this one, I thought. Probably old and classic.

"You seem to travel a lot, sir."

"That I do, Jesse. One of our plants is in the Silicon Valley and one in Irvine. I shuttle between them. But sometimes I wonder if it's worth it, being away so much from the family. I'm lucky if I see them on weekends. It puts a lot of responsibility on Mrs. Eichler."

"I guess that's the price of success," I said, trying to sound as if I understood and was around success myself a lot of the time.

"You know my son, Wilson?" he asked.

I kept my eyes on the pickup truck in front. There was a little brown-and-black terrier loose in the back and I was afraid he might leap out. I couldn't bear it if I killed something.

"I only met your son once," I said. "At the party." Wilson had been bombed, I remembered. He'd been making a castle of champagne glasses.

Mr. Eichler sighed. "That awful party. I wish to God Wilson had never had it."

"I know." Another "if only." "But it wasn't the party

that killed my brother, Mr. Eichler. You don't have to feel responsible about that."

He leaned forward and looked into my face. "You're a nice boy, Jesse."

We'd just about run out of things to say to each other and I was glad to see the beach parking lot.

Bunches of people still milled around and the police car still smoldered. A fire truck was pulled to the side.

Mr. Eichler told the cop who stopped us that we'd come for Chloe's car.

"You just go ahead and get it, sir," the cop said.

I could imagine what would have happened if *I'd* come to pick up her car. It would have been a repeat of the security guard's attitude in the airport parking.

"Are you sure it's OK for you to come back and stay with Chloe?" Mr. Eichler asked.

"It's OK."

"The club's only a few minutes away, Jesse. You can call us if you're concerned."

I guess he must have been feeling a bit guilty about leaving because he kept on explaining. "This is our party, you see, and we've invited three other couples to join us. We're returning hospitality so it is a little difficult."

"I understand. We'll be fine." Returning hospitality with a dinner at the club was a new one to me but I figured it must be important. One thing I knew, though. My parents wouldn't have left Bry or me at night if we'd had emergency treatment in the afternoon, not for something ten times as important. Which didn't mean Chloe's mother and father didn't care about her, I suppose. They were different, that was all. They had different priorities.

I drove back to the house behind him.

Chloe had changed into a soft, yellow robe and her bandage was covered by an oversized white sock. She lay on the couch with her foot on a cushion.

"I've taken one of the pills already, Jesse, so I'm going to be great company," she said. "I'll probably fall asleep. You'll be bored to tears."

"No, I won't." I could look at her if she fell asleep. It would be like watching her through the binoculars, taking my time, touching her with my eyes. The thought made my face warm. I'd never be bored looking at her. "Is it OK if I call my parents?" I asked Mr. Eichler and he waved a hand at the phone. "Help yourself."

Dad said they'd heard about the riot and he was glad I'd called, and no, they didn't need the car tonight. They weren't planning on going anywhere.

"Any word on the posters?" I asked.

"Two calls. I passed them on to Officer Valle."

"What do you think?"

"I don't have a great feeling about either of them."

"Oh. Well, I won't be too late."

Mrs. Eichler took me into the kitchen then and showed me a platter of cold chicken and salad makings in the refrigerator and a crusty loaf in the bread drawer.

"I'd put it together for you, but we're late already," she said.

I smiled at her. "Besides, you're not exactly dressed for the kitchen."

She smiled back, that small stretching of her lips. Here in the overhead fluorescent light I could see how much stuff she had on her face. I decided I liked faces better when you could see them. She and Mr. Eichler made sure I had the club phone number and that I understood Chloe couldn't have another painkiller till 10:00 P.M. They thought they'd be back by then.

"Dad?" Chloe said. "Be careful, OK?" She glanced at me and I knew she was thinking how easy it is to lose someone you love.

"We'll be careful, honey. Don't worry."

"And Mom? Be good."

"I will." It was the kind of thing two sisters would say to each other and it made me smile.

"They're nice," I said, after they left.

She nodded. "And now, let's you and me make a pact.

81

If you promise not to keep asking me if my foot hurts, I'll promise not to whine. Not unless it does."

"Deal."

I sat opposite her in a velvet chair with a matching stool, leafing over a magazine, not talking so she could rest. The stereo was on at some light, classical station, and a small sea breeze moved the soft drapes at the open French door. Now and then we'd hear the bang and sizzle of firecrackers, and once the night outside burst into crimson stars that crackled as they melted into darkness.

"Do you need to call and cancel that date?" I asked abruptly, not looking up from my *Surfer* magazine, turning a page nonchalantly.

"I did already. Anyway, it wasn't a date. A girl called Cinnamon Balfour's having a beach barbecue and Kevin Vohs was taking me."

"I know Cinnamon Balfour. I went to that school, too, you know. Before you did."

"That's right. I forgot."

"Cinnamon Balfour. Brownish hair. She was a junior."

"She became a senior."

"I guess. I remember Bry used to play tennis with her some Saturday mornings. He said she was good. She beat him a couple of times."

"You had to be good to beat Bry. I never could. Cinnamon was really upset about Bry. She was at the funeral."

"Oh."

I leafed over some more pages. Never in the history of the world had *Surfer* magazine been read with such unseeing eyes.

"Was it OK with that guy, Vohs?" I turned another page.

Chloe shrugged. "Of course it was OK. He was taking a bunch of people. He was probably glad of one less."

She had her hands clasped behind her head and her eyes closed. I could glance up in the quiet without her knowing. Hair, blue-black in the lamplight, eyelashes shadowing her cheeks. Her mouth. I wondered about Vohs. Did she like him? She opened her eyes, caught me looking at her, and smiled that heart-stopping smile. "Hi!"

"Oh, hi!"

She smiled again. "Want to go out on the deck for a while and watch the fireworks? We can see the whole beach scene from there."

"Sure." I jumped up. "Need any help?"

She swung her legs to the floor and I helped her stand, keeping my arm around her as she hopped to the French door. Maybe I should have offered to carry her, or better yet have swept her up. Get real, Jesse! What do you think this is, *Gone with the Wind*? I pulled the drape all the way back and the night air came in, cool and fresh and smelling of seaweed and firecracker smoke. There were two chaise lounges with cushions on them and I helped her into one.

"Does it hurt a lot . . ." I began and she stretched up, put her fingers against my lips and took them quickly away again.

"Remember our pact? I'm not whining, am I?"

"Sorry." I leaned across the railing, still feeling the touch of her fingers, knowing myself muddled and embarrassed and happy. How could I be happy? I shouldn't be. It was too soon to be happy and certainly not here, with her.

Below was the bulky darkness of Clambake Point and beyond that the ocean, polished by moonlight. Bonfires dotted the dark strip of beach and there were people, small as beetles. The white lightning of a sparkler flickered and there was a shower of green stars that fell silently above the waves.

"Oh, look!" Chloe sat straighter and pointed and I saw a sailboat coming round Clambake Point, its sails outlined in red, white, and blue lights.

"Nice." I sat on the other chair next to her. "Are you warm enough?"

"Not really."

I'd seen a blue blanket on the back of the living room chair and I got it and tucked it around her. We sat close and quiet, watching the fireworks explode below us. Our boat drifted across the darkness. The sky was filled with shooting stars, and I knew I'd never forget the magic of this Fourth of July night, here with Bry's girl.

12

Chloe shivered. "I think I'd like to go in. It *is* cold. You don't have to."

"That's OK."

We got up at the same time and somehow I bumped her, not her foot, thank goodness, but her arm, and she swayed a little, and I caught her and we were standing very, very close in the breezy half dark. She wasn't cold. I felt the heat coming through the yellow robe and I could see her eyes and her lips that were slightly parted. I could smell that perfume smell of her, and somehow, without even knowing how it happened, I had my arms around her and hers were magically around me and we kissed. Her mouth was cool and salty.

"Oh, Chloe." I touched the smooth darkness of her hair, trailed my fingertips down the curve of her throat.

"Oh, Jesse!" Her voice teased. "Now don't get too excited and step on my foot."

I let her go and moved back.

"I didn't mean you to *retreat*," she said and the teasing,

mocking, tender note was still there. "Come back. I'll put my foot in my pocket."

I stared at her.

"What's wrong? Now don't start saying you're sorry you kissed me, because it's OK."

"It's not OK. It's too soon." I leaned over the railing again. The outline of the little boat with its colored lights was blurred. I tried to forget the feel of Chloe's mouth.

"Why is it too soon, Jesse? Because of Bry? I liked Bry an awful lot, but not that way."

I was shaking my head. "He thought you liked him that way. He was building a dream on you, Chloe. You were his hearing girl."

Her voice shook. "Can we go in the living room? I have to sit down."

I helped her inside and onto the couch. "Should I close the door?"

"Please."

She was sitting up, so when I came back I carried the footstool over.

"I want to tell you about Bry," Chloe said.

"I don't want to hear, Chloe. Not now."

"He was so brave. He didn't go around making a big deal out of being sorry for himself. He *did* things, like playing soccer. I mean, how hard to play soccer . . . Anyway, when I saw he was beginning to like me too much maybe I should have stopped him, but . . ."

"But you didn't. Because he was deaf. You were sorry for him, is that right?"

I began pacing, picking up an ashtray, putting it down, examining carefully a china figure of a girl on a swing.

"Yes. That *is* right. You don't believe me?"

"I do believe you. I was sorry for him plenty of times myself." Times when he was younger and kids made fun of him and called him dummy and mocked the way he talked. I'd punched out a few of them. Not when Bry was looking, though. Not when he'd know.

"I never ever showed I was sorry for him," I said.

"Well, I didn't either. Don't you see? That's what made it so hard. I didn't want him to think I was turned off because he was deaf. He'd had enough things hassle him all his life because of that and it wasn't the reason. I liked him the way I liked other friends but it wasn't special." She was biting her lip, looking down at her foot. "I'd decided . . . because he was beginning to say things . . . and I was noticing . . . I was going to tell him that . . . and then the awful thing happened."

The awful thing! I had to get away. I put the china girl carefully on the table. "I think I'd better get you something to eat now, Chloe."

"I couldn't eat."

"You should, though."

The flourescent ceiling light in the kitchen was too bright when I switched it on. It made my eyes ache and they were aching already.

I filled two plates with the food in the refrigerator, poured lemonade, and put everything on the tray Mrs. Eichler had left out.

Neither of us seemed to be hungry.

"Bry told me . . ." Chloe began once and I interrupted her. "Could we just not talk about Bry anymore? Not to-night."

Chloe put down her fork. "Jesse? Are we never going to be able to be friends, because of Bry? Do you think that's what he'd want?"

"I don't know, Chloe. He's dead and I can't ask him."

I sat miserably then, moving the food around on my plate. Why had I jumped on her like that? She hadn't done anything wrong. I struggled for words to make things halfway right again, but I couldn't find them. "It's just . . ." I began.

"Sure. I know. It's just." Chloe pushed away her plate and picked up the remote control for the TV. There was a program on Channel 28 about whooping cranes. We watched in silence as they rose heavy and white into the air, so beautiful they made my throat hurt.

Halfway through, the phone rang and it was Chloe's

mother and Chloe talked to her. "Yes, I'm feeling OK." She glanced quickly at me. "But pretty soon I'm going to take another pill and go to bed."

"I am truly exhausted," she said to me when she hung up. "I think I'll go now. Thanks for everything, Jesse, and you don't have to stay. My mother says they're leaving in a few minutes."

"I'd rather stay," I said.

"Good night then."

"Goodnight."

I moved to help her but she said quickly, "I can manage." So I watched her go.

She stopped at the bend in the stairs. "Will you call me sometime?"

"Yes. But not for a while."

"I don't think I'll hold my breath," she said.

There was a rerun of "Brideshead Revisited" on and I sat and watched that, sat in the chair where Chloe had been, with my head where her head had rested. I tried not to think of her upstairs.

Pretty soon her parents came. They were real early and Mrs. Eichler ran upstairs right away to see how Chloe was, while her dad thanked me again for staying. I could smell alcohol on his breath, not foul and ugly the way it smelled on Plum's breath. This was sweetish and pleasant. Probably expensive stuff. Probably wine.

When her mother came back she said Chloe was almost asleep and I tried not to think too closely about that either, about that dark head on a white pillow, the shadows of her eyelashes on her cheeks.

I said I'd be going then, and they both thanked me again, and I walked down to the street where I'd left my car. After I unlocked it and got in, I sat, looking at the house. The dark window above the porch was Chloe's room. I could see the corner of the deck where we'd stood together and kissed. What had I meant when I'd said, "not for a while?" How long was a while? Long enough for me to forget Bry? But I never would. I lay back and stared at the roof of Dad's car. It was cold and I was cold. Time to go.

I had the key in the ignition when a car turned into Sapphire Cove Road, its headlights moving like searchlights across the Eichler's front yard, across the driveway, across the house, moving on, leaving everything in darkness. Lionel Richie's "Dancing on the Ceiling" crashed behind it as it roared on toward Clambake Point.

I sat, stunned, my heart thumping.

I'd seen something in those headlights, something that filled me with so much dread that I'd started to shake. I opened the glove compartment, my hands jumping so I could hardly pick up the flashlight Dad keeps in there for emergencies. Noiselessly I opened the door and went back up the Eichler driveway. From inside came the faint voice of the newscaster. Eleven o'clock. At eleven o'clock the Strathdee sisters always take Fluffy down to the gates at Del Mar. They'd seen the car. I turned on the flashlight and hooded it with my hand.

Chloe's Mustang was pulled in front of the closed garage door and beside it was Mr. Eichler's Volvo. Old, he'd said. Probably a classic, I'd thought. It was a shining dark green with a curved back, a 122S, probably 1966 or '67. It must have been in the garage when I brought Chloe home or I would have noticed it. My heartbeat was trapped inside my chest, thumping to get out. I crouched at the back of the car, shone the light low. Old-fashioned splash guards, rubber, black and shining and perfect like the rest of the car. In the middle of each was a white circle with a V inside. V for Volvo. I clicked off the flashlight and stayed in my crouch. Everything flooded back—the screech of the brakes, the thump, my brother dead.

"You'll remember," Officer Valle had said.

I remembered.

13

IN THE EICHLERS' living room the TV blared out a commercial for American Express. Still crouching I ran to the front of Mr. Eichler's car and felt along the fender. Nothing. I examined the hood, my light moving small as a tennis ball across the perfection of dark green paint. Nothing. But when I let my hand follow the light I thought I felt a slight concave dip.

"These little foreign jobs bust a gut if you even look at them," Plum had said. But not a classic well-preserved 122S Volvo like this. This car was built.

I checked the tires, pushing my fingers into their pattern. I'd bet a million dollars they'd match.

What if I marched up to that front door and confronted them? And Chloe would hobble from her room and . . . What if I went to a call box and had the cops march up with me? They wouldn't, of course. They'd want hard evidence.

"Chloe's parents were at a party in Newport Beach," I'd tell Officer Valle. "They were drunk and they drove home and changed their minds and went back. Remember, those tracks going both ways?"

Bent over, I ran for my car.

There's a turnout on the ocean side of Coast Highway between Clambake Point and Del Mar. I drove in and cut motor and lights.

All this searching and suspecting and it had turned out to be Chloe's father! And he'd seemed so nice, so real. My stomach hurt. How would Chloe feel? But maybe it had been someone else, some rotten turkey who'd borrowed his car, panicked after the accident, and put it back. No. The car that hit Bry had gone along their street, past their house to Clambake Point. That would be too big a coincidence. It was their car. Wilson? No. We'd left him at the party. Someone had driven this car the other way first. Someone. Mr. Eichler! I rolled down the window and breathed in gulps of cold air. God! What was I going to do? If only there had been someone who'd *seen*. I needed a witness before I started accusing.

Sowbug! This time I had to find him.

I rammed out onto the highway, slowing, because there are always dangerous drivers on the roads and this was still the Fourth of July. But I had a hard time concentrating on being careful. My mind kept jumping and the car jumped, too. It would feel this way to be driving drunk. I slowed some more. Easy, Jesse, and stay cool. Above everything, stay cool.

From the Del Mar overlook I could see that Sowbug's place by the tunnel was still empty. I got out and walked, scanning the sand that was deserted now except for a group still celebrating around a roaring fire. It was cold, with a sharp night wind off the ocean. Even the seabirds had found shelter somewhere. Sowbug wasn't here. OK. There were other beaches to check. I'd checked them before; I'd check them again.

I drove to Scotsman's, to Aliso, to Corona Del Mar, to Huntington. I stumbled over lovers, illegal campers sacked out in sleeping bags, walked around a dead and stinking seal, and all the time my mind seesawed, trying to hold a balance. I remembered Mr. Eichler at Bry's funeral. Did

91

he sing? Did he pray with the Reverend Orville that Bry would find peace? Or did he pray that he'd never be found out?

I drove to Bolsa Chica.

Mrs. Eichler had thought the posters were a practical idea. I imagined her telling her husband, "Don't worry. Nobody saw," and I choked down my rage.

Sowbug wasn't on Sunset Beach. Nobody was on Sunset. Could he have gone north? He'd have had to have a ride and if he did he could be anywhere, clear up in Ventura County even. I turned south, freewaying till I got to the Dana Point turnoff, then cutting toward the beach again. There was still plenty of action around Doheny where all the big motor homes were parked. Once Mom and Dad and Bry and I rented one of those and went fishing at Lake Cachuma.

I went on down to San Clemente and San Onofre before I turned. No Sowbug. Talk about the needle in the haystack, whatever that was. It was twenty minutes of four when I was cruising past Webster Beach. Four in the morning always seems the downest time there is. That's when I waken to memories of Bry, to the heartsickening thud, to the loneliness of that bedroom, empty next to mine. I bet there are more suicides at four A.M. than any other time. I wondered if Mr. Eichler ever wakened at four A.M., if he lay sweating, reliving as I did that final thump of metal on flesh.

The parking lot at Webster was empty, the yellow lights shining ghostlike on the dark concrete. They're constructing a new fishing pier and at the same time doing something with the sewer lines. Big, concrete pipes are strewn on the sand and I slowed some more, getting that sudden rush of blood through my veins, hearing Officer Valle's voice, "Sowbug likes tunnels he can crawl into." Yes!

I peeled into the empty parking lot and jumped out. The wind plucked at my sweat shirt and blew my jeans against my legs. Jeez! I'd never felt anything as cold as that wind. But I had something else. A need. Once I knew, once we had Eichler, the pain would stop. The emptiness would be filled.

There was a bundle of rags rammed in the mouth of the first pipe. The bundle didn't close it all the way because those big concrete tubes were maybe five feet in diameter. I poked the rags out, knelt, and shone my light inside. There were two mounds of clothing way in the center of the hollow tube. One of the mounds moved.

"Sowbug?" The tunnel echoed my voice but only mine.

I tucked my flashlight under my chin and began crawling. The cold came up through my legs, into my stomach. And my stomach wasn't feeling that great anyway.

I reached the first lump and shone my light. The man was round and gray-whiskered and pale as death. He was not Sowbug.

The second lump was a woman wrapped in layers of clothes, her head on a stained satin pillow.

"Lemme alone," she muttered and I quickly turned off the light.

It was hard to back up and I had to crawl over the man again. "Sorry," I said. "Excuse me."

Outside I stayed on my hands and knees, letting the sickness ebb. I hadn't thought about how it was. "Sowbug, I'll never again . . ." I said out loud. But I didn't know what I'd never do.

Another pipe. Another bundle bunched in its end. There was nothing to do but make myself face it. When the packing came out, bits of clothing scattered around my feet. There was a dirty red-plaid shirt that looked a lot like the one Sowbug wore.

I shone the beam inside, and there he was, alone in the pipe under his torn blanket, curled up with his arms around his wine jug.

"Bug?" He snored and curled himself tighter.

I reached in and shook his foot, but not as hard as I once would have shaken it.

"Bug? It's Jesse Harmon. Wake up. I need to talk to you."

He tried to pull his foot free and squirm farther into the pipe, but I had a firm hold and I slid him out toward me. It was like pulling a dog out of a hole. But he wasn't a dog.

"I'm sorry, Sowbug," I said. "I'm desperate or I wouldn't do this to you."

He lay in the sand, boneless, shading his eyes and face, making one last effort to wriggle away.

I held on and shone the light in my own face.

"Don't be scared, Sowbug. I'm not going to hurt you. Remember me? Jesse? From Del Mar Park? It was my brother who was killed. Here, sit up. I'll help you."

His blanket had stayed behind in the pipe. I fished it out and wrapped it around his shoulders. He still had the wine jug, about an inch sloshing in the bottom. If he was too drunk to talk I'd wait around till he sobered.

"Let's go to my car," I said. "It'll be warmer. Come on, Bug."

He didn't want to go anyplace, but I pushed him ahead of me through the soft sand. Partway up he unscrewed the top of the jug and drank as he walked. I took the empty jug from him and dumped it in the trash basket. Then I wedged him into the passenger seat, got behind the wheel, and started the engine.

"We goin' someplace?" he asked.

"No. We're just going to sit here and talk." The heater came on with its little roar. I decided to let him sit for a minute and thaw before I started my questions. It didn't take long for the car to start smelling pretty bad and I had to roll down my window a couple of inches. I heard him snore.

I prodded his shoulder. "Sowbug! Dammit, don't you go to sleep on me." I shook him some more. "The car that killed my brother. You saw it happen, didn't you?"

He stayed limp, but I sensed the minute understanding came, when it got through to him exactly who I was and what I wanted. I sensed the sudden wariness.

"I don't know nothin' . . ." The whine was back.

"Yes, you do. It was a dark green car, right? A Volvo,

94

1966 maybe. I even have the registration. All I need is a description of the man who was driving it."

He drew in his breath in a wheezy whistle.

I began guessing. "You were up poking around in the trash, just at the entrance to the beach that night, and you saw Bry get hit. Right? You didn't know who it was. I believe that, Sowbug. If you'd known it was Bry you'd have gone to help."

He nodded vigorously. "I sure would. I would have helped."

"And when the car stopped, you were right across the highway." I was visualizing it, reliving it again though I didn't want to, and suddenly I knew exactly how it had been. "And the man had to step out to reach Bry's shoe." I opened my door, put my left leg out, reached across the hood with my left arm, pretended to throw. "Like that?" Tears closed the back of my throat. "And you were just across the highway and you saw him," I said again.

"I didn't know it was your brother, son. I swear it. I would have helped."

"You can help now. Just tell me what the man looked like."

"The police. That Officer McMeeken. I don't like him."

"You don't even have to talk to him. I'll arrange it. Officer Valle is nice."

I'd closed the door again and it was very warm. Sowbug shucked his blanket. "They won't take me in?"

"No."

"They won't make me leave California? That Officer McMeeken said they'd ship me to Alaska if they ever found me sleeping on the beach. . . ."

"He's only trying to scare you. Tell me about the man."

His lips twitched in a smile. "That weren't no man, sonny. That was a girlie."

"A girlie?" Immediately the image of Chloe flashed in my head, Chloe in her blue swimsuit, smiling for the camera.

"Yes, sir. Nice looking, too. Fancy dresser. Classy."

95

I swallowed. "You eyeballed her good, Sowbug?"

"Yeah. The parts I could see. Saw her back. Saw a fair piece of leg as she stepped out. Worth seeing, too." He was chortling and I wanted to slap him, new understanding or not. A woman! "Heels this high, and one of them sexy gold chains around her ankle. Saw clear away up above her knee when she put her . . ."

I leaned forward. "A chain?" I couldn't believe what he was saying. "A chain, Sowbug? Did it have a diamond in it?"

"Can't say. But I'd know it again. I'd know that leg, too."

I grabbed his wrists. "Now, listen, Sowbug. This is major. Are you sure the woman was driving?"

"You saying I don't got eyes? You saying I was drunk? You insulting me, boy?"

I tried to get my head together.

"So the man was on the passenger side?"

"There weren't no man. That little lady was in the car all by herself."

I sat back, stunned. Someone *had* taken the car. Chloe's mother had taken it.

14

I DIDN'T SLEEP at all that night. At seven on Sunday morning I was out on my surfboard, still trying to put things together, and worse, trying to decide what to do. I found myself wishing I had Bry to talk with. Yeah, sure! Smart thinking, Jesse.

There was no doubt that I'd tell the police. But should I tell my mother and father first? I couldn't bear not to have them know before anyone else. But suppose I was wrong? I owed it to Chloe's mother to be sure. I *was* sure. I owed her nothing. Did I owe Chloe anything, Chloe who'd been Bry's girl, my girl? Chloe who was her mother's daughter? Should I break it to her before the cops did?

The wind was straight offshore and the waves were pumping. I caught a big, fast left, carving on the inside of my rail. The speed felt good. For a few seconds I was able to blank out everything except the green tube I was in. The blankout didn't last. I paddled back slowly into the lineup and bobbed for a long time, making my decision.

But Mom and Dad had left for early church when I got

back. Mom's note said, "I'm sorry you aren't with us, Jess. Breakfast's in the oven."

I turned the oven off and called Chloe. It was her mother who answered and I had a hard time even speaking.

"We want to thank you again for staying with Chloe last night," she said.

"You're welcome." Cold, sarcastic voice. Couldn't she sense I knew? How could she have faced me these past days, spoken my brother's name? She'd passed the test, that's why. I'd been in her house and she'd probably been scared at first, but she'd passed the test and every day she'd felt safer. She hadn't wanted me to stay last night and she'd been right. *Well, you're not safe any longer, lady.*

There was a long pause before she said, "I'll get Chloe." Had I imagined that pause?

"Jesse?" Chloe's voice came almost immediately. She sounded breathless, as if she'd hurried. "Oh, I'm so glad. I'd decided you wouldn't call, and then I thought maybe you would, just to ask about my foot. . . ."

I'd forgotten about her foot. "How is it?"

"It doesn't hurt as much."

"Good." There was an edge of something pink showing under the coffee table and I bent and poked it out. It was a little plastic windup mouse that Bry had brought home one day. Wind it up and it turns endless somersaults. I held it, rubbing its silly pink head.

"Could I see you, Chloe? I want to talk to you now."

"Sure. I'd love it. Come on over. I'm stuck here, but . . ."

I didn't want to talk to her in that house, in her room with her mother downstairs.

"If I walked over could we take your car and go to the Point? I'd drive."

"Great." There was a flicker of worry in her voice, though. She was picking up on something. Last night I hadn't wanted to talk. What had changed?

"I'll be there in fifteen minutes, Chloe."

98

I walked quickly, almost running past the place on the highway.

Soon now, Bry.

The dark green Volvo was still in the driveway, Chloe's Mustang beside it. Mr. Eichler opened the door when I rang and I wondered if he knew, if his wife had told him, if he was covering up, too.

"Come in, Jesse," he said.

"No, thanks, I'll just wait out here." And then, because I couldn't help it, I added "Nice car."

"I like it. Well, if you're sure you won't come in I'll get Chloe."

It was a minute before she came. She wore a pale blue sweat suit and one grubby white Reebok. Her smile was enough to stop my heart in midbeat. She, or someone, had drawn a Snoopy face on the oversized white sock on her bandaged foot.

"Hi," she said.

"Hi."

She held my arm going down the steps. Behind us I sensed her mother in the hallway and I turned and let myself glance down at her ankle, at the chain glittering and sending off its hard little sparks.

"Jesse?" that was her voice.

I looked at that mask of a face with all expression enameled over.

"What?" My jaw was so tight that I could hardly get the word through it.

"Nothing," she said.

Chloe and I sat at Clambake Point looking over the gray toss of sea and I told her.

"No," she said.

"Yes. It was your dad's car. I'm certain the tire tracks will match. I'm certain we'll find your mom's prints on Bry's shoe."

"My God. What shoe?" I will never forget the horror in

99

her eyes, the way she covered her mouth with her hand when I told her.

"But it couldn't have been Mom." Her chin trembled. "I was so relieved that it couldn't have been her. She and Dad drove home together that night, and the next day when we heard about Bry, I went to Dad and I was scared and . . ." She was crying soundlessly, her face wet with tears. "He said for me not to go imagining things, just because . . . he knew for sure it wasn't Mom."

She stared out of the window, whispering words that I couldn't hear. One fist pounded her knee.

I waited. She sighed, closed her eyes. "It *was* my mother. I can see that now. She had a headache when she came home. I remember, she took aspirin. I asked Dad if she'd been drinking and he said only one. He keeps an eye on her. She hates it but he always does. He said she'd had a headache all night. She'd lain down on Mrs. Levin's bed for a while." Chloe turned so all I could see was the back of her head, her hunched, hopeless shoulders. "She'd have had a bottle hidden somewhere, of course. Dad checks her purse but she must have got it past him."

"She'd take a bottle to the party?"

"Probably it was a half pint. Nice and flat. Slipped down inside her bra."

I couldn't figure if it was anger or despair I was hearing in Chloe's voice. "I'll bet she drank it, lying there on Mrs. Levin's bed, and it wasn't enough, so she thought she'd just slip out and drive home. We find bottles hidden in the weirdest places."

"She'd drink half a pint of whiskey and still try . . . ?"

"Probably vodka. My mother likes vodka best, if it's available. If not, anything will do."

"She'd drink that much and still get in a car and . . . ?"

"When we lived in Palo Alto she rammed her Toyota right through the back garage wall, thinking it was in reverse, and she was drunk at my eleventh birthday party and . . ."

"Don't, Chloe," I said. "What's the use?"

"And when we were little, nobody would car pool with us because they knew, and Dad would make all kinds of excuses when she was too bombed to go places. He'd say she had flu. And we moved a lot."

Chloe wiped her eyes with the backs of her hands. "It's our fault, too, of course. Mine and Wilson's and Dad's. Mom hides her drinking the way she hides everything else about herself. We help her hide it. I'm so sorry, Jesse. But sorry isn't enough, is it?"

"Couldn't you see she was a death waiting to happen, Chloe? Like Plum? Couldn't you see? Why didn't you *make* her get help?" I moved away as far as possible, till my back was against the door. She was right. They *were* all to blame.

"You think we don't try? There's no way to make her go. Dad even fooled her once, introducing her to a counselor, hoping they'd get friendly. It didn't work. Mom says she doesn't have a problem. She says alcholics are sickies and have no self-control."

My leg jerked, my knee bumping the dash, and Chloe quickly moved her Snoopy foot out of the way.

"What's she going to say now?" I asked bitterly. "Is she going to say sorry, too? Just don't ask me not to go to the police, Chloe. Just don't ask."

Chloe shivered. "No, I couldn't. Not after what happened. But please! Let me tell my dad first. OK?"

Three kids in a van with Idaho plates pulled in next to us. A bunch of surfboards were piled in the back. "Hey, man," the driver called. "Where's the best waves around here?"

"Try down the highway," I said. "Trestles."

"Thanks." They were gone.

Chloe and I sat silently. A fog was drifting in, blotting out the horizon.

"I don't think they'll find any surf," she said tonelessly. "It's glassing over. Oh, Jesse! I wish we could run and run. Just the two of us . . ."

"There's no place to run." I started the car. It was eleven o'clock and my parents would be home.

* * *

I'm working now at Taco Bell, and Debbie Green and I are dating, but nothing serious. We were in Penguin's Frozen Yogurt one night when Chloe came in with some guy. I'd imagined seeing her again and I'd tried to prepare for it but I wasn't prepared.

"Hi, Jesse," she said.

"Hi." The word scratched my throat. "How are you?"

She shrugged. "Did you know that my brother has joined the navy?"

"I didn't know that."

She nodded. "He figured out how to run away. Wilson always does."

That was all, except that my palms were sweating and there was an empty hurting ache in my chest.

"Isn't that the daughter . . . ?" Debbie whispered.

"Yes." There would always be whispers about Chloe now, whispers about all of us. Everybody knows about Mrs. Eichler. The papers are full of it. How she'd left the party when she was supposed to be resting. How she'd driven home and found her house filled with kids. How she'd turned the car around and killed Bry. It's hard for people to accept that a hit-and-run driver can be rich and respectable. And that an alcholic isn't always a bum drinking wine out of a bottle in a paper bag.

The Captain says the Eichlers will be ruined financially and that Mrs. Eichler will go to jail. She should. She killed Bry. But I don't want to think of her in jail. I know they'll be ruined more than financially, and I don't want to think about that either.

It's strange. I'd been so sure that finding that driver would make me feel better. If anything I feel worse. I'd thought all my own "if only's" would disappear. It doesn't work that way. The pain doesn't stop or the emptiness fill that easily.

Mrs. Eichler wrote us a letter begging our forgiveness. "I've had trouble looking in your eyes, Jesse," she said.

"I've had trouble looking in my own. I am screaming inside."

We are all screaming inside, Mrs. Eichler. Mom and Dad, and I.

My dad doesn't talk about what has happened. He goes fishing a lot.

I went with him, one hazy, early morning. There was a heavy swell and we sat out there with our lines dropped into the gray bulge of water.

There were things I needed to say to him.

"Dad?" I began. "I keep thinking that maybe I could have saved Bry somehow. I can't get away from that. If I'd jumped forward. If I'd . . ." I reeled in my line, keeping my eyes on its tight shine. "I saved myself, Dad."

He was quiet for so long that I thought he wasn't going to answer. Then he said, "I don't know what to tell you, Jesse. No use saying you'll get over it. You probably never will. You'll live with it, and your mother and I'll live with our guilts, too, and if we're lucky they'll dim a bit as the years go on."

"*Your* guilts? What do you mean your guilts? You weren't even there."

"We were there for all of Bry's life. I don't know if we did the best for him. We never encouraged him to be different or to think of himself as different and we thought we were handling things well. But was that right or wrong, Jess? Was it for Bryan, or for us?"

"You mean because he talked instead of signing? That was right, Dad. Shoot, Bry talked so well nobody would have guessed, or not for a while, anyway." I fumbled around in my head, looking for words to help. "And that time the Hearing Center people sent you and Mom to Denver to that big meeting to tell how . . ."

Dad interrupted. "And those deaf kids were there, carrying placards about deaf pride and signing how we hadn't let Bry have any. I remember all right. He didn't sign. He never learned and we didn't either. Bry wasn't a part of that world—or of the hearing world. Where was he, Jesse?"

The float bobbed below the surface and Dad stood and yanked so hard on the line that the rod arched like a bow. I saw the strain in his arms and face. He freed a clump of monster seaweed, tossed it back in the ocean, and sat again, staring across the dreary water. "Everybody's left with something to regret, Jesse. We just have to go on the best we can."

"I guess." I hadn't told Dad how I'd been thinking about Bry's girl just before that car hit him, ten seconds before that awful, sudden silence, and that I had that guilt to live with, too.

Mom has become ultrareligious, and not only on Sundays. Mrs. Daniloff brought up another of her good casseroles and a leaflet about a support group called Together.

"They've all lost a child to violent crime," she told Mom. "They help each other come to terms with it."

But Mom just shook her head.

"I don't think she's ready yet," Mrs. Daniloff whispered to me. "I'll try again in a couple of months."

I'm not sure if Mom will ever be ready for that. Maybe religion is her support group. Maybe she and Dad have each found their own kind of amazing grace.

We gave part of the reward money to Mothers Against Drunk Drivers and part to a ranch that works with handicapped children. There will be a new Bryan Harmon bunkhouse. The Newport businessman donated his part of the money to a job project for homeless alcoholic men. I told Sowbug about that, but I don't think he wants to go. He likes the beach.

Officer Valle says there's nothing she can do about Plum.

"You can't take away a license without proof of a crime, Jesse, and you can't help someone who doesn't want help."

Chloe had been right about that. But I guess her mom will get help now whether she wants it or not.

In two weeks I go back to school.

Sometimes at night I go into Bry's room. I sit and I stare at his trophies, his books, the surfboard in the corner that's as dead as he is, and I promise myself that I'll never let go of his memory.

It seems impossible that there'll ever be anything between Chloe and me. How could there be? Her mother, my brother. I've started work on her clock, though. Grandpa and I discuss clock problems on the phone, but he hasn't asked me what I'm going to do with it when it's finished. I don't know myself. Finishing it is going to take a long, long time. I just have to hope that by then, I'll know.

About the Author

EVE BUNTING was born and educated in Ireland and came to the United States in 1959 with her husband and three children. She has written more than one hundred books for children and young adults since her first book, THE TWO GIANTS, was published in 1972. Among the many awards Ms. Bunting has won are the 1984 PEN Los Angeles Center Special Literary Achievement Award for her contribution to children's literature, the 1976 Golden Kite Award, and the 1977 Southern California Council on Literature for Children and Young People Award. Ms. Bunting currently lives in Los Angeles, California.